Already over 50 5star Reviews for the Island of Serenity series.

5 ***** Reviews from Book 3, The Island of Pleasure, Vol 1

"**This was my first read from this author**, but won't be the last! Read it all last Friday without a break. I love the style!"

"**You'll surely enjoy this book!**"

"**Awesome book** and you will feel the excitement all throughout while reading this book. Quite long story however you will never get bored cos of the twist on every scene of each character. Great to read and can't wait for volume 2."

"**The storyline is realistic and believable!** Loved the characters and the story was very interesting."

"**Beautiful and Exciting Read!**

"**I loved the twists and turns of this story** and I love fiction. The storyline is so engaging and I love how the characters unravel themselves into the plot. I This was such a great book. I recommend this to all those who love fiction, drama and romance novels."

"This novel is such an interesting blend of intrigue, suspense and challenges to the protagonist's identity- a masterpiece!

This novel, 'The Island of Pleasure' is creative in the extreme and offers the reader a refreshingly interesting new concept, showing originality and skill from the writer, Gary Gedall. Words and phrases leap out of the page, and like a magician, the author creates suspense and intrigue as the reader is swept along through powerful dialogue, and expert characterization. It actually reads a little like a film script and the characters seem to be so in charge of the plot, that we can forget at times about the author at all. This is a very modern novel, filled with language which is richly opulent, as the concept of pleasure is unpacked by the author, in this third part of his 'Island' series.

What comes to mind is John Donne's quote, 'No man is an island entire of himself....' and this compelling book focuses on interaction in a very specific way, spoken language being a pivot that cleverly compels the plot into being highly active and mood driven. The emotional potency of this book specifically offers a backdrop to the action, as Faron experiences a new world which he feels challenges him on certain levels. Without spoiling the plot, this is an existentialist type book, which on the other hand in a post- modern way plays with stereotypes, even right down to the titles of the chapters; 'Showing The Cat Her Claws' is an example of the literary blend of alliteration, with every day connotations and associations that make this novel appealing universally to readers of any sort of educational background.

It is a well-crafted book, exploring the human condition from several different vantage points, and notably it is filled with questions which the reader gains an insight into the entire world of the writer's imagination through.It is an accessible novel, focusing on universal experiences yet offering a plot that is highly unusual and fascinating.

The sensory language employed skillfully in the novel, makes the encounters that Faron goes through ones which the reader is also lead on in a an almost interactive manner, as the reader embarks on a journey of revelation and enters into the dynamics that Faron's desires take him on.

The clever exploration of Faron's strengths and weaknesses make him seem at times a hero, and at other times, someone with a sense of being driven by his sense of adventure, alone in a world in which he experiences encounters that sometimes seem surreal."

"This third part takes us to a Venice sometime in the past and Faron, the (anti)hero, is in charge of a high class brothel. Again, the darker side of the man is exposed, with all his fancies and desires, which are often selfish and manipulative.

As with the other two books, the author succeeds to draw us into the complex thoughts and feelings of his man, making all his actions and choices seem reasonable, if not totally obvious.

The writing is as always rich and absorbing, I really felt like I was there, with him, making all those choices. He is both hateful, lovable, but mostly understandable, I love the way that these books are written."

"… **The way the characters were depicted** within the novel and flow of story truly amazed me. This novel is really unique because the writing is descriptive and makes it easy to perceive the emotions of the characters and visualize the narrative aspects within. I have also read the other previous books, which are also amazing and amazed me with their romantic flow. I really enjoyed reading this book because it touched my soul with the flow of a beautiful romantic story. This book kept my interest from start to finish. Wonderfully insightful and compelling book, I truly have never read anything like this before. I am happy that I have this mesmerizing book."

I like this novel, The Island of Serenity, not only because of the romance involved but more so is the lesson behind the story. Wow! I never really thought I would enjoy this kind of reading. I am not a fan of romance fiction stories because I perceived it to be boring, but hey! I was all wrong. This book is one of a kind, it really kept me reading the entire day. With the twists of the storyline, my eyes were really glued on every page, until I never realized it's already about to end. What a great, exciting read it had been!"

"The series is really quite unique, I don't think I have read anything quite like this before and I am enjoying it immensely. There are so many twists and turns in the storyline that you are always wondering just what will come next"

"**Well written journey of Faron** filled with twists and turns as the reader feels right at his side. A completely engaging story and all relationships are intertwined perfectly.

Gedall is a highly talented writer who deepens the exploration of humanity and projects his perspective in a unique story. Look forward to the next volume. His thoughts and ideas with Faron's journey are complex and deep but in some ways full of simplicity. Highly recommended."

"**The Island of Serenity Book is not quite like anything I have read before,** crossing genres and constantly surprising as the story, and what we know of its world, continually develops and expands. The author delivered an interesting and fascinating world with bold and memorable characters. I found the writing compelling, a real page turner."

The Island of Serenity

Part 1

Book 3

Pleasure

By
Gary Edward Gedall

07 03 2015

Published by

From Words to Worlds,

Lausanne, Switzerland

www.fromwordstoworlds.com

Images synthesized by Boris: contact@avasta.ch

ISBN: **2-940535-13 -2**
ISBN 13: **978-2-940535-13-2**

About the Author

Gary Edward Gedall is a state registered psychologist, psychotherapist, trained in Ericksonian hypnosis and EMDR.

He has ordinary and master's degrees in Psychology from the Universities of Geneva and Lausanne and an Honours Degree in Management Sciences from Aston University in the UK.

He has lived as an associate member of the Findhorn Spiritual Community, has been a regular visitor to the Osho meditation centre in Puna, India. And as part of his continuing quest into alternative beliefs and healing practices, he completed the three-year practical training, given by the Foundation for Shamanic Studies in 2012.

He is now, (2014 – 2016), studying for a DAS, (Diploma of Advanced Studies), as a therapist using horses.

His hobbies are; writing, western riding and spoiling his children. Quora writer of the year 2015

He is currently living and working in Lausanne, Switzerland.

Realization, Repentance, Redemption, Release & Rebirth

This book was inspired by the realization that I had never really mourned the death of my older brother, Lloyd, to whom series is dedicated.

In my therapy practice, I am all too often confronted with patients who feel that their lives no longer have any sense or perspective.

It is my job to help them find back the sense of their lives, and to encourage them in finding again some optimism that things can get better.

This book is for all of you that have made errors, mistakes, stupid and destructive choices and actions, (which should cover approximatively 99% of the world's population).

We have all got it wrong sometimes in our lives, but it is never too late to start to get it right.

Any form on self-harming, or life threatening acts are a crime against yourself; your God, (however you might name or experience 'it', even if you are feeling totally abandoned), and everyone that cares for you, (and there are always many more than you might feel at any moment).

Remember, you can always find teachers; therapists, spiritual and religious guides, etc., etc,. who are there to help you on your path. If you need help, don't hesitate to reach out, you don't have to face your demons alone.

I take also this opportunity to thank my daughter, Kyra for her help in the structuring of the series, and the time and interest that she invested in reflecting with me on the stories.

Disclaimer:

The characters and events related in my books are a synthesis of all that I have seen and done, the people that I have met and their stories. Hence, there are events and people that have echoes with real people and real events, however no character is taken purely from any one person and is in no way intended to depict any person, living or dead.

Contents

1.   Take a pair of sparkling eyes

It is suddenly much colder; Faron wraps himself as best he can in his flimsy seeming cape.

Much, much colder here than on the first island, the cold wind glides over the dark sluggish canals, scoops up a fine spray of icy particles, spraying his delicate, exposed face, and lashing his brown almond eyes with freezing droplets of sarcastic tears.

'Where are we?'

'As I have already said, this is Venice', replied the heavyset, grey haired gentleman, patiently.

'But how did we get here?'

'I seem to remember something about quite a lot of pills and a not insignificant amount of alcohol'.

'I know about that, but how did we get here from the other island, and …,' he examines his elegant, manicured hands, 'I'm human again.'

'Because the beast has been calmed; you have learned all you need for the moment about survival, and so you are now here. Here you will learn about pleasure.'

'Are you serious?'

'Young man, pleasure is a very serious business. I wonder if Mae West ever said that?'

'Then lead me on, Macduff.'

'May you see things well done there'.

The older man turns and starts to lead off into the night.

The handsome, young Casanova has to run to catch up with him.

They are traversing one of the many bridges that criss-cross the dark arteries and veins of this islands city.

'Wait, wait, where are you taking me?'

'To a palace of pleasure, don't you want to go?'

'Sure, sure, why not? But, but is it like some sort of hotel or brothel?' His voice easily expresses his concern.

'Yes, I'd say, something like that.'

'But, but,' he hunts frantically in the pale blue silken costume, 'I don't can't find my wallet, or any money or even a credit card.

How am I going to pay for anything? What sort of sick game is this, are you going to lead me to somewhere and leave me broke?'

'Faron, what would be the point of embarrassing you in that way? How could that possibly teach you anything about pleasure?'

'So do I have a credit line or something?'

'No, it's like Pleasure Island, everything is free'

'Pinocchio nearly turned into an ass on Pleasure Island.'

'Then you have little to worry about, do you?' And with that rather stinging remark, he turns again, nimbly jumps off of the bridge and back onto solid ground.

The dark green figure is in danger of disappearing totally into the shadows when Faron choses to catch him back up.

2.   The Great Western Europa & Regina Hotel
San Marco 2951

The fiery torches of the side entrance welcome the two.

As they enter, a man appears as out of nowhere, deftly steals their capes and immediately disappears back into the shadows.

'What the …?'

'Do you want to be dragging round your cloak all night?'

'It's just ...' He stops to peer into the distant room,

'what the …?' He repeats, for the second time.

'Something wrong?'

'Sort of.' Without waiting for his escort, he hurries along the gloomy corridor and enters into an immense ballroom.

It must have been quite splendid, like Hippolyta on her nuptial hour; the rich red flock wallpaper, great paintings on most of the walls, rows of gilded mirrors and a ceiling worthy of the Sistine Chapel.

But as with even the most beautiful of brides, time bleeds away their beauty, like a hungry Skeksis squeezing out his daily dose of life essence.

The walls are worn and wane, the mirrors browned and liver spotted, the pictures, like the hitherto magnificent ceiling have lost most of their colour, like an old tattoo, where only that uninteresting, muddy green stamp remains.

The furniture, more easy to damage, but also to replace, is in much better condition, following the intricate crimson and gold style of those that wish to impress.

The men are all in silk and lace, as are the wonderfully, beautiful ladies, the main differences being; that the ladies all have impossibly, intricate hair styles and the men all wear half masks.

These masks are all fantastic works of art; diamonds and coloured jewels, feathers and bones, gold, silver, electric blue, bloody red, jaundice yellow and beetle green.

Will Scaramouch suddenly declare himself and fence his way out, cutting a bloody and humiliating swathe, both with blade and tongue, each sharper and more cutting than the other?

Another lackey appears, again, seemingly from nowhere.

'Buona sera, signore Ferguson', and before Faron has a moment to react, the man is covering his eyes with the most ornamental of all the masks, and then, bows, and is gone.

'What the…? And how does he know my name?'

'But this is your establishment, locally known as the posto di Ferguson, the Ferguson place.'

'This, this is, this is my place?'

'You do catch on quickly, don't you?'

'But then I can anything that I like?'

'You are here to learn about pleasure, and this is why you don't need any money, everything is already yours.'

'But, but what about the girls?' Faron's attention has already wondered over to some of the particularly attractive girls, dancing or chatting with the men, or amongst themselves.

'Well, slavery is no longer practiced here, although they do all work for you, indirectly, so you would have problem choosing any of them for fulfil any particular service that you might desire.'

'Any particular service that I might require', he repeats mechanically, he then surfaces a moment.

'Indirectly?'

'The girls are under contract to a certain signora Nicola Mallevaichi, she is what you would term as a Madam.'

'But I can still …?'

'She is your associate, you work together, the girls could be considered as one of the many perks of your position.'

Faron smiles a slight, tight smile, bows slightly to his companion, turns towards the assembled revellers, grabs a glass of fizzing champagne from a passing waiter and heads towards a pretty brunette that has caught his eye.

3. Morning has Broken

It is still relatively early, eight thirty three to be exact.

The grey haired gentleman, locally referred to as signore Guida, is sipping a latte macchiato. A half-eaten bignè al cioccolato, patiently awaits to join its other half, inside the dignified gentleman's ample stomach.

Faron sweeps majestically into the gilded, breakfast room. He wears a black, silk dressing gown, discreetly adorned with fiery, golden dragons.

For someone that has had only a few hours of sleep and having consumed an impressive quantity of champagne and assorted cocktails, he seems surprisingly fresh and spry.

'Good morning, my good man.'

'And so it seems to be.'

'It's incredible; pissed as anything, not much sleep, must have screwed half a dozen of the tramps working here, and I wake up like I'm on a boy scout camp.

And …,' he caresses his face, 'it's like I've just had a shower and shave, but I just woke up like this.'

'You are here to learn about pleasure, Faron, and that you shall.'

'Well, I'm certainly enjoying my first lessons.'

'Exactly, your first lessons,' he tips the remainder of his stained milk between his smiling lips, grabs the last half of his chocolate donut, and eases himself off of his chair. 'I'll leave you to it, then. Enjoy this first part of your lesson.'

'First part? What other parts can there be?'

'This is just, how can I say it? This just the antipasti, the main course will follow in due course.'

And then he is gone, leaving a very troubled Faron, but not for long, for a hearty, and tasty breakfast awaits him. Not to ignore the evening to come, and then the rest…

4.   There's a Light, over at the Ferguson Place

Night after night, night after night,
We stuck, nor breath nor motion;
As idle as a painted ship
Upon a painted ocean

'I'm bored'.

'What can we do for you, signore Ferguson?'

He had eaten and drunk everything that he could think
of and desire, and just until he could neither eat nor
drink any more, and that only from sheer exhaustion.

He had slept with every girl of the house; once, twice,
five times. He had had them every way, front, back,
face to face, 69, one, two, three at a time.

They had made love to him, to each other, he had
kissed them, fondled them, slapped them, beaten them.

He had dominated them and tried being dominated by
them, but the interest, thrills and excitements had
quickly faded, the green, ugly stain, was all that
remained from that beautiful dream of pleasure.

The painted faces of the pleasure girls, concerned that their host would be angry with them, seemed no more to belong to real, human girls, than the cast masks that the male patrons wear to protect their good names.

The storm rages outside, thrashing the windows with whiplashes of wild, wetted wrath. La Piazza, (San Marco), must be already six inches under water. Fifteen centimetres of ugly, brown flood, just waiting to wheedle its soggy way around the sandbags into the stores and cafes around the famous square.

'Ahem.' Faron turns to the maggiordomo, 'there are two young people at the door. They are looking for a place to spend the night. It seems that the gondola in which they were travelling capsized and they lost all their belongings, including all their money.'

From his tone, it is clear that his appreciation of the validity of their tale, leaves something to be desired. Faron is already gesturing for him to send them on their way, when something stops him.

'Wait, show them in, let's see what they look like.'

Two, very wet and very sorry looking people, slop their way into the ballroom.

'And just who might you two be?'

'I'm Rad, and this is Janet. We're here in Venice, on our honeymoon,' and, as if she had forgotten that, she suddenly turns to her new husband, grabs at his shirt, as if she was about to drown, and bursts into heaving fits of tears.

'There, there, I think that you are both wet enough already, we don't need to have any more humidity in here.

Yes, yes of course you can stay, in fact you must stay, I absolutely insist. Marcus', he turns to the major Dom, 'you will take Rod…'

'Rad'.

'Yes, Rod, up to my room, run him a hot bath, and give him something comfortable of mine to wear.

You,' he points at one of the girls, he had never bothered to remember any of their names, 'you, take her up to your room, bath her, dress her in that red dress that I like, and do something about her face and hair.'

He then turns back to the couple, 'dinner will be served at nine, you are my special guests. … So, what are you all waiting for?'

No-one has moved; but now, the two honoured guests are being shepherded up the wide, gilded, ornamental stairs.

As he turns back into the room, he softly instructs, but to no one in particular, 'ready the hounds, the hunt is about to begin …'

5. Food for thought:

The table holds a mini banquet, the white Faenza plates
and dishes, are beautifully offset by the golden strands,
deftly spun into the exquisite Venetian glassware.

There are small glass, crystal hand bowls, so as to able
to wash one's hands, at any moment.

There is a boiled sturgeon centrepiece, decorated with
Faron's own coat-of-arms picked out in garlic and red
sauce. On ornate, heated plaques, there waits a
sturgeon fish, a roast course of wild boar and other
meats to be accompanied by red wine.

There will be nine courses for the meal and each course
will have eight different dishes. They will include
antipasti, trout patties and pike spleens.

The folo scalco, banquet organizer, hovers
majestically, overseeing every minute detail. Il
trinciante, the meat carver waits patiently, his knives,
razor sharp and at the ready.

While the bottigliere, is already busy, serving Faron a
fine, full bodied Tuscan wine.

Faron should be savouring the famous wine, but he is
not, for he is bored. He has been offering himself the
same banquets for weeks now.

Everything starts to smell and taste the same, no matter
what it is.

Just like his sexual boredom, he is now also ennuyé by
the food and wine.

He is trying his own patience, waiting for Rad and
Janet to join him at the table, waiting for these two
Zed's to appear and breathe some life into his now
Apathetic, bored body.

Suddenly, the mini orchestra ceases its rendering of a
Scarlatti aria, to be replaced by a Vivaldi sonata, the
folo scalco, orchestrating the evening from a vantage
point, somewhere a little 'off stage'.

The base rhythm of the harpsichord perfectly underpins
the footfalls as they descend the elaborate staircase,
step by step. While the violin and cello follow the
gentle swishing, to and fro of the long, red taffeta
dress.

She is having quite a difficult time succeeding to keep her balance; she would have been wedged into tight, high heel pumps, tied into this restricted, corseted, twisted, woven gown and yet, now is expected to glide, effortlessly down this rather steeply inclined stairway.

He, was doing all that he is able to help her, all the while trying not to slip on the highly polished steps, due to the smooth, leather soles of his intricately patterned slippers.

His apparel is less difficult to navigate than hers, the silks and satins, are still, after all, in most aspects, no more than an elaborate long jacket and short, tight pants.

'Welcome, welcome my most honoured guests', Faron is on his feet almost immediately. 'Come, come and join me here.'

He comes to shake their hands; Rad, rather rigidly takes the preferred object, and pumps it up and down, as if trying to suck water, up from a rusty well.

She, timidly takes his hand, while using her other arm
to cover and protect her almost naked chest. The
décolleté of her dress is particularly low cut, and the
effect of the ties is to push her breasts, up and out.

To be crudely honest, the design of the garment is
intentionally to push the breasts as much up and out of
the dress as possible, but all the while keeping the
illusion of fashionable elegance.

'Please sit,' he gestures Janet to a place next to his own
chair, Rad to take a seat at the opposite side of the
table. The guests, too intimidated to refuse, follow his
seating plan.

'There's really a very lot to eat.'

'No problem Rod, you can have a doggy bag, if you
want'.

He doesn't reply, just wonders if his name is
mispronounced deliberately or not.

'What might we serve you, M'lady?'

'Well, you know, if I'm to wear these types of dresses, I can't eat much'.

'Nonsense, you can eat as much as you fancy, and you won't gain even a gram. And as for you,' he turns to Rad, 'you can drink as much as like, get totally rat assed, stay up 'til five, six o'clock. In the morning, you wake up like you've drunk a hot milk at ten p.m. and slept all night, so drink up.'

He gestures for the camerieres to start to serve the food, and so the festivities commence …

'What is this custard, it's wonderful?' Rad had been drinking quite heavily all through the meal. The bottigliere had been particularly attentive to never leave the guests' glass empty, and his attentions were now showing their effects.

'It's usually known as Zabaglione, but here in Venice, we call it Zabaio.'

'Well it's bloody excellent.'

'Then have some more, have as much as you like. And bring some cantucci, you can dunk them in into the Zabaio.'

'Is it meant for that?'

'Actually I usually dunk them into my Holy Wine'.

'Holy wine?'

'Yes, Vin Santo, Holy Wine, great with cantucci, almond biscuits.'

'Sure, let's try that as well.'

'Your husband seems to have relaxed a bit.'

'I'm sure that he is just tired.'

'Don't worry, I'll see that he is well taken care of.'

'But that's my job, I'm his wife.'

'You have the rest of your lives to be his wife, tonight, you are my guest.'

6.   The chase:

They sit for a moment in silence.

'I think that I should go to bed.'

'But you are not tired'.

'But I must.'

'Why must you?'

'Because it is late'.

'And you need to be up early tomorrow morning?'

'Yes, yes, that's it, I must get up early tomorrow morning?'

'But how silly of me, of course you do. You mustn't be late for work'.

'Work?'

'Are you not going to work tomorrow morning?'

'Of course not, silly, I'm on my honeymoon.'

'Why, of course you are, how very silly of me. It's because you have a river taxi booked.'

'No, no taxi booked?'

'Hair appointment?'

'No.'

'Nails?'

'No.'

'Teeth?'

'No, don't be ridiculous.'

'Okay, then I give up, why do you have to be up early tomorrow morning.' She hesitates for a moment.

'It's none of your business.'

'Ah, but there you are wrong, it is totally my business. You see, as your host, it is my sacred duty to see that all your slightest wishes and desires and fulfilled.'

'And if my desire is to go to bed, is that not your job to fulfil that wish?'

'Madam, this establishment is my business, and like all good businessmen, I am skilled in imagining what the client actually wants, even when they refuse to accept that desire for themselves.

If you only knew of how many men have come in here for a very particular form of sexual favour, only to find themselves unable to ask, nay, unable to admit to themselves, their true fantasies.

But it is my role to dream into their requests and to seek out the hidden treasure, like a sandworm burrowing for spice.

You Madam, have no wish to achieve your boudoir, no, quite the opposite, what you want more than anything is to stay here with me, only you are too frightened to take the risk.'

'Risk, what risk are you talking about?'

'What do you think?'

'That, that, that you might attack me, force your attentions on me.'

'Liar! How dare you lie to yourself so blatantly!'

'I'm not lying to myself, how dare you!?'

'Come, come,' he makes the merest nod to the bottigliere, who whispers in between them, silently refilling their crystal goblets, 'you expect me to believe that you think that I, Pierre-Alain James Faron Ferguson, would imagine to force myself on you, my honoured guest?'

'Then why won't you just let me go to bed?'

'Because, dearie, you haven't yet finished your glass.'

'And when I've drunk this, will it be okay for me to go to bed?'

'Just don't Rumple that dress, it is very special.'

'I don't follow you.'

'But you will.'

'Only if you a clearer.'

'Oh, I am very clear, it is you that is unclear.'

'Maybe it's the wine.'

'Yes, you could be right. Sambuca, my good man. It is not usually served as a dessert wine, you know, but I don't always follow custom. Those three objects floating of the top, are coffee beans, they are supposed to denote good luck.'

The drink must have already been pre-ordered, as it arrives almost instantaneously.

'But I don't want any more to drink, I've had enough.'

'It is considered as likely to bring very bad luck if you do not swallow the beans and drink the wine.'

'What rubbish.'

'I think with losing your ride and all your belongings is already bad enough luck, and to take the risk to lose this beautiful lodgings, with the, as-much-as-you-can-eat, menu option, would be the very worst of luck.'

The subtle threat hits home, but on a more subliminal level, as Janet didn't seem to react at all to it, however…

'Why not, you any live once'.

'Some say that you only live twice.'

'What's that meant to mean?'

'Private joke'.

'Well, if we only live twice, maybe I should have another one of these?'

'Looking for some more good luck?'

'There's more?'

Faron knows that it was now her turn to play with him, but he would wait to play his trump cards, sometimes by losing a battle you find a new way to win the war.

'Luck is where opportunity meets preparation.'

'Another private joke?'

'No, someone once said it. Come, I want to show you something.'

'No, what, wait, I don't think that …', the moment of confidence has slipped back into its deep hole of habit, leaving only the slightly anguished, nervous young woman, who usually inhabits this body.

'Come, please, I promise you that I not do anything that you do not totally wish for me to do.'

'Promise?'

'I give you my word, and the word of a Ferguson, is stronger than steel, it is made from girders from Scotland, please come.'

She gently lowers, then raises her head. He offers her his hand, she makes an uncomfortable gesture with her other arm to try to cover her, all too exposed chest.

'Why are you so embarrassed by your body?'

'I am not embarrassed by my body?'

'Then why do you keep trying to cover it up?'

'It's just, just that…', she drops her arm from her breasts, grabs the glass and swallows the rest of the liquid gold. 'There', she consents to allow him to ease her up.

She is not used to wearing such high heels, nor to drinking so much, but with a determined chin, she organises, chest, arms and legs, and stands proudly facing the man.

'Come, the night is warm, I want to show you something.' He gallantly offers her his arm; after only the shortest moment of indecision, she accepts, and they gently glide out of the sala da pranzo, through the adjacent hall and towards the massive ballroom.

However, that is not his objective, he leads her through a single door that leads under the gilded staircase.

The passage is quite narrow and she is slightly pressed towards his hard, elegant body.

He exudes confidence and assurance, this is his domain. Outside, before, in that other world, his first life, he had failed. He had compensated for his deep lack of real assurance by using the money and power that he had benefitted from his father.

He remembers threatening that boy at school with the menace that his father would sack the boy's father if he didn't do as he wanted.

It seemed that all that he was, was nothing more than the borrowed trappings of his honestly powerful father.

No more than a little girl traipsing around in her mother's high heeled shoes, always in danger of falling, as the shoes were clearly much too big for her all too little feet.

Here, now, living twice, he is the master of this castle, 'Ferguson's place', where there is always a light, always food, always wine, women and song.

Yes, here and now, he is the Master, this is the island of pleasure, he can have anything that he wants.

And now what he wants is Janet, and having acquired confidence in the magic of this world, he knows that he will have her.

Of course, he really could force himself on her, there would be no consequences, but rape is no longer interesting for him.

He had tried that experience on some of the girls, the first few times he had felt a certain omnipotence, but like everything else here, the feeling didn't last for long, and boredom quickly engulfed him once again.

No, here it was the chase that was 'worth the candle', as his mother would say.

'Just through here', he leads her out, outside to a walled garden. Alpine lilies and pansies, crocuses and primroses, are growing in profusion in wild abandon.

'Why, it's beautiful,' she moves to run to smell and caress the Tiger lilies, ensorcered, by the magical golden on gold petals, but almost falls head first onto the blue-grey and white Carrara marble slabs underfoot.

'Careful', he smiles winningly at her, and leads the delicate flower to a double sized, cushioned letto.

He gently lowers her down onto the comfortable daybed, thankfully, she relaxes onto the soft upholstery.

'Thank you.'

'I am only here to serve you.'

'Really?' she smiles back up to him.

'Of course, and now, just to complete the moment …'

From somewhere, neither too close nor too far away comes the sweet strains of 'Goodbye my Asian Flower', and from somewhere even closer comes a decanter of sweet smelling almond essence.

'To the most exquisite flower, in the whole of this garden.'

'Don't you think that I've had enough to drink already?'

'I have long ceased to think, and as for alcohol, as I am already totally drunk with the nectar of your very presence, it is just a pleasant taste on my lips.'

She demurely takes the proffered glass and takes a very long and slow sip.

She is getting drunk, and she knows that she is getting drunk, but we all know that there is a moment when we knew that we are getting drunk, but because we are getting drunk, knowing that we are getting even more drunk, doesn't succeed to do anything to stop us getting even more drunk.

'And that is all that you wish to take pleasure for your lips?' She is pushing him, she knows that she is pushing him, she knows that she shouldn't be pushing him, she knows that she is finding this incredibly exciting.

'I think that you should go to bed.'

'Why?'

'Because you have had too much to drink and you do not know what you are saying.'

'Of course I know what I am saying.'

'You are not really attracted to me, you are just aware that Rad is going to be the only man that you will sleep with for the rest of your life, and you now realise that you haven't really had as much experience of other men as you would have liked.'

'I have never slept with any other man.'

'Then dearie, you will never know what you are missing.'

'Maybe I should not know.'

'Quite right, off to bed.'

'It's not for you to send me off to bed.'

'No, you are quite right, taking you to bed is not my right. It is Rad, who now commands you.'

'Rad does not command me.'

'But he is your husband, it is now his total right to tell you what to do and what not to do.'

'Nobody has the right to tell me what to do. Least of all you, I would like another drink please, and I will stay here as long as I please.'

'But what would he say if he knew that you were here, with me, alone, drinking Amaretto by moonlight, in a beautiful flower garden, with you lounging seductively on my day bed?'

'It would be absolutely none of his business. So you think that I am lounging seductively?'

'You're trying to seduce me, aren't you?'

'Not at all, I'm just relaxing, enjoying the evening?'

'…And my company?'

'You're okay, I suppose.'

'Then would it be acceptable if I was to sit here, next to you?'

'Of course, I've nothing to be worried about.'

'But what would I say to Rad, tomorrow, if we ended up kissing, tonight?'

'You would tell him nothing, that is the sign of a gentleman.'

'And you would be comfortable keeping such a secret?'

'My life is my own, married or not. Is there any more in that glass thingy?'

He gets up, searches out the decanter and refills her glass. He watches attentively as she drinks.

'What are you looking at?'

'I am so sorry, how rude of me, I was just lost for a moment. I was watching your mouth, your lips, just thinking for how very beautiful they are.'

'You want to kiss them, don't you?'

'What man wouldn't?'

'And what would you give, for just one kiss?'

'Only my heart, only my soul, nothing of value, not diamonds nor coal.

I gave you my all, I give what I can, but is all is for nothing, I'm only a man.'

'Well, maybe if I add the free room and board, I suppose that, that should just about do.'

She leans down onto the cushions, her hand slips over the edge of the sofa, gently releasing the empty glass onto the delicate stone.

He slides up towards her head, one arm reaching behind her neck, the other gently encircles her waist.

But he does not kiss her, no not just yet. He allows his small, beaked nose to gently caress her soft, scented neck, then, following surely behind, his ready lips and tongue. Like cat at the cream, he licks up her milky, white skin.

The roughness in his tongue on her neck sends electric shivers down her spine. She grabs the material under her hands and crunches it up into a ball in her now sweaty palms.

She lifts her neck, accepting the eternal damnation which is to come.

His fangs unsheathed, he goes for jugular, but refrains from drawing first blood. The night is still young, he must savour the moment before that irrevocable penetration.

He drags his head away, finally giving room for her to twist herself towards him, and bury her thirsting lips and tongue deep into the power of his meaty mouth.

His right hand travels up her demanding body, skims the scanty covering only to plunge into the hot, softness of her waiting breasts.

The dress seems to have been cut specifically so that they can be unveiled at the smallest gesture.

He slides her towards the interior of the bed, and himself straddled over her, grabbing her bare breasts between both his broad hands.

The nipples are already hard and extended, under, her heart is beating a royal tattoo, it's time to call out the troops.

They are not big, nor round, nor particularly pert, but they are now his, his to pull, the squeeze, to suck, to lose himself within.

Every touch, stroke, squeeze, causes a quiver of thrill, of pleasure, of excitement.

She grabs his neck with her flying arms, pulls him up and closer to her, she needs his mouth again on hers.

He flattens himself onto her body and she can now feel him, hard and present.

She rubs herself in excitement, pleasure and anticipation.

She reaches down to take his hand and directs it towards her thigh. Following her lead, he now has both hands around her thighs.

The dress is cut so that the part below the waist is in two halves, one at the front which overlaps the part at the back.

To see it worn, this couture construction is not obvious, but its purpose becomes clear in this type of circumstance.

They circle around the back, squeezing and releasing her tight, little buttocks. She starts to arch and relax with each squeeze, tightening and releasing her pelvis and pubis.

His hands slowly start to reach round to the front, 'why is he taking so long? I want him. I want him to take me.'

Then they stop, violently grab hold of her slip, and then rip it down and off. As if released from some modern day chastity belt, she pulls up the loose front of the dress and opens wide her legs.

The tender peach has bloomed and juiced, now only waiting to be picked and devoured. Sliding his greedy hands back up and in between her legs, he opens the soft skin to suck and savour the sweet nectar from the swaying stigma.

She wants him; it is wonderful, it is electrifying, her body quivers with each thrust of his tongue, but it isn't enough.

She must have him, she must hold it, stroke it, caress it, consume it. It needs to be in her hand, in her mouth, in her vagina.

She twists herself downwards, her hand grabbing for him.

He knows well this gesture, he releases her, slides onto his knees, opens his pants and displays his manhood.

At least that was something that worked before, even if during the last few years, it had become increasingly difficult to attract and sleep with women, it had always worked beautifully.

Well maybe, admittedly not so well after he had starting drinking heavily and gained all that weight.

Now, that was all behind him, now he is in peak condition, on all levels. He can manage it almost none stop, he had had five or six girls in one night. No, that wasn't true, there was that orgy, when he might have had nine or ten. – Things became less clear as the night wore on.

He can feel her thrilling under him, she grabs for it, holding it tightly, it seems that she is undecided about just what she wants to do with it first.

But of course that didn't matter, he is about to take his kill. 'Okay, dearie, it's time for some special magic ....'

7.   Debriefing and Re-briefing

'Just couldn't do it.' They are gently strolling down the Riva degli Schiavoni, they are going to have a late breakfast in one of the pasticcerias in the Piazza San Marco, the guide had expressed an aching need for a freshly baked krafen.

The day is dull, overcast, windy and generally, pretty miserable, there had been rain, there is likely to be more.

'Why do you think that you couldn't?'

'She wanted it so much, so wanted me, but yet we both knew that the pleasure was wrong. She was my Trilby, and I just wanted her to sing for me, I didn't care about her at all.'

'So you think that you understand her?' Turning into San Marco, Faron is suddenly hit by a freezing gust of wind.

'Understand a woman, good God no. I know how to handle a woman, but what goes on inside, Lord no, that's the biggest mystery in the world to a man.'

'Here take this.' He hands him a long scarf that Faron wraps thankfully around his head, face and neck.

'Would it maybe help in some way if you understood women better?'

'Sure, and just how might I do that?'

'And are you sure that you don't want anything to eat?'

'Well, I had breakfast not long ago, but funny now you think of it, I'm suddenly starving.'

'Yes, I thought that you might be, but unfortunately, we have a little problem.'

'What sort of problem?'

'Well, you see when we are in your place, we don't need any money but …'

'Come off of it, this on only some sort of a dream, I don't really need any money, I could just go and take whatever I want. After all, this is the island of pleasure. I can do anything that I want.'

'Well actually, really, no. You see Faron, you are here to learn certain lessons, and to learn these lessons, then there are certain rules.'

'What rules?'

'Like if you want a coffee and doughnut, you'll need some cash money.'

'Screw that.'

'Well that's the way that it is.'

'But I'm fucking hungry.'

'Then maybe you should see if you can find someone to ask who might advance you some lira.'

'Fuck this!' Faron turns away irritably from the older man, only to see J.J. and Maman just standing in front of the church.

Of course they don't look exactly like before.

J.J. is wearing, what must have been an expensive yacht jacket, yet it is now quite worn on the elbows and cuffs, and it is much, much too big for him.

He had clearly been quite fat when he had bought it, but now he is looking quite cold, thin and miserable.

Maman, on the other hand looks superb; her clothes are chic, well fitting, and expensive looking. She has a long woollen coat and is wearing a slightly ridiculous hat, quite high and full of feathers, which often attract the attention of the famous pigeons of the square.

Faron approaches them confidently, but as he approaches, they make as if to not notice him, and continue unheeded with their conversation.

' … it is easy for you, you have the most beautiful girls that line up to work for you.' He continues.

'It is my job to train them into the art, I care for them, feed them, clothe them, teach them all that they need to know, so as to be the very, very best in the whole of Italy.

Why else do you think that I have such a wonderful reputation?' She is, as always, the stronger.

'I still hold that it is because you have the material to begin with.' He is not quite ready to concede.

Faron, feeling cold, hungry and increasingly irritated, steps forward and confronts his parents, who somehow seem to be somewhat taller than he remembers.

'You know, other people exist you know.'

'What do you want, baggage?' J.J.is even more irritated.

'Don't you call me a baggage. What do I want? I'll tell what I want, I want some money to go a buy myself a coffee and a doughnut.'

'Well you'll get nothing from me.' He continues.

'I should have known better than to ask.'

'Here', she starts to hunt in your jewelled bag, 'I've some coppers for a street urchin, we girls have got to stick together, don't we now?'

And so she gives Faron the handful of small coins.

Totally confused, he takes the money, but before he could even to think to thank her, J.J. has thought to continue the conversation.

'Now, if you were to take on someone like that brat, now that would prove to be something.'

Faron, not understanding much, cash in hand runs off towards a little cafeteria on the corner of San Marco and Calle Canonica.

On passing the window he glances at himself, not much to notice; same coat, seems somehow a bit bigger, baggier than before, weird thought.

The scarf covers most of his head and face but it is the same almond shaped, eyes and eagle nose that reflect back at him.

One strange thing though, he seems to feel some sort of tight band, attached around his chest, pulling his shoulders slightly back and up, again weird.

He goes into the bakery, once protected from the bitter Venetian wind, he unwraps the scarf and loops it untidily around his neck.

He waits his turn to get to the counter, now feeling terribly hungry and thirsty.

'Yes miss, what can I get you?' 'Is he mad, or this some strange type of joke?' Either way, he is too hungry to argue.

'I'll have a milky café and chocolate doughnut please.'

'With pleasure', he smiles at Faron in a slightly too friendly way.

Faron takes the coffee and cake towards an empty table in the corner. 'Curiouser and curiouser, the world just grows more curiouser.'

On passing he glances again at his reflection in the café window and only just manages to not drop his tray.

'Oh my God, oh my God', for looking back at was no longer Faron, but someone else with the same almond shaped, eyes and eagle nose that reflect back at him.

… It is Aideen.

8   Curiouser and curiouser

Yes, it truly is Aideen!

The shock, as one might imagine is quite extreme, he, she, or what-ever, stands for a long moment trying to take in the image.

It is surely Aideen that is staring back at 'him', reflected in the café's vast window, all the more clear due to the overcast day, threatening more desolate rain at any given minute.

People are trying to pass, people are trying to get to the empty, corner table that Faron had noticed and was heading for, people were try to take Faron's space.

It is that basic territorial instinct that spurs him into action, and he, blocking the way with his body, manages to seat himself before the other customers can invade this, particular expression, of an Englishman's castle.

He sits, huddled over his coffee and cake, surprised by the smaller, dainty hands that handle his cup and carefully break open the Italian doughnut, spooning out the rich, chocolate cream filling with his teaspoon.

Then something strikes him, he never eats this with a spoon, this is not his way to eat breakfast.

It reminds him of being a prehistoric hunter, there were abilities and senses, even, dare one say, knowledge and memories, that didn't belong to Faron, but to him.

Is this not the same? Being transformed into this strange body, would he also gain certain knowledge and traits, that are private to her, but not to him?

Strange body? But no, this is not a strange body, this is Aideen, Aideen, his own flesh and blood, Aideen has lost daughter, Aideen, one of the people that he loved the most in this or any other world, Aideen the person that he had succeeded to screw up, more than any other.

'So here I am, struck in my own daughter's body, but not even,' he strolls over to a steamy mirror and inspects his, her face. 'She must only be sixteen or seventeen, maybe eighteen at most.'

He returns to the table and finishes up his breakfast.

'So what do you do now, 'young lady'? ', he asks himself. For want of any better plan, he replaces the scarf, buttons up his overcoat, as the wind is free, and heads back towards the hotel.

Knowing full well that if neither of his parents recognised him for who he is, or even as Aideen, there would be little likelihood that he would still be offered open house at the Ferguson place.

9. In just seven days ...

Faron arrives outside the familiar great doors, but has lost his confident manner of ringing the bell to be admitted. He takes a deep breath and rings the bell.

The few moments seem like an eternity, the door then swings smoothly open. A sort of familiar face is discovered on the other side.

'Oh Mike, thank God, please, please can you let me in?'

'Do I know you?, And it is not Mike, my name is Marco', but just the same, he seems troubled by the familiarity of the young urchin girl, standing on the threshold.

'Who is it, Marco?' But before he gets the opportunity to answer, Faron rushes past him and up to the elegant lady standing in the hallway.

'Madame, you met me at the square, you were kind to me, you gave me some money, please, please, please can you help me?'

Faron is not used to grovelling, and is a little surprised to hear himself behave in this manner, but does nothing to stop himself either.

'So you have chosen to accept my little wager then?' J.J. has suddenly appeared by her side.

'No, she just came like that, unannounced.'

'So you refuse to prove yourself?' He is obviously enjoying goading her.

'No, I don't refuse to prove myself, I stand by my word, as always.'

'So you believe that you can pass off this baggage, as one of your girls, in just a week?'

'She would have to accept to do absolutely everything that I tell her to.'

'I have to accept what? I'm a good girl I am, I won't do 'anything' that you tell me to.'

'There, there, young lady, don't you worry, she won't ask you to do anything wrong, just to smile and talk to the gentlemen that come here to relax.'

'I know what this place is.'

'Madame, will you promise that you will not ask this young lady to do anything indecent or immoral?'

'I said that I could pass her off as one of my girls, none of them have ever been forced to do anything more than be friendly with the men. What-ever else they might choose to do, is always their own choice. Some girls do, some girls don't, some girls need a lot of loving, and some girls just dance and tease.'

'There you go, nothing to worry about. You'll be well looked after here, and I'll see to it that nothing bad happens to you.'

'You, sir are a gentleman.'

'Abate a poor one.'

'That is until you find your duke, and marry Casilda off with him.'

'My daughter has been betrothed to the duke's son since childhood, and even though we have had no contact with him or his family for nearly twenty years.

Now that the old Duke James has passed on, his son is heir to the title and to all his lands.'

'Even though you don't even know his name or where-a-bouts?'

'I have been reliably informed that the family nurse came here to Venice, with several large bags, and even that she is still supposed to be living here in Venice.'

'But if the Duke has chosen to hide away his offspring, it would have been for a very good reason, and not for us to go meddling in his affairs.'

'If his parents chose to hide their children away, for fear of assassination, that doesn't change anything. He is dead now'

'And you are sure that the hiding was not out of fear of marrying their son to your daughter?' She mocks.

'I don't understand.'

'It is not your business, young lady.'

'Sorry, … sir.'

'So, what is your name?'

'Aideen, ma'am.'

'So Aideen, I am willing to offer to you full room and board, AND the best education in the whole of Venice, no, the whole of Italy. I will teach you how to be a lady. You will do everything that I tell you to, without question or hesitation. If you do that, you will be well looked after, if you don't, you will be beaten and thrown out back into the streets.'

'Madame?'

She turns and smiles to the man, 'figuratively.' She turns, and shouts up the stairs, 'signora Guida, please come down stairs.'

A fat, older woman, wheeze's her way, asthmatically down the great staircase. Faron does a double take, it is the same person as the old gentleman, who he left only an hour or so ago, so it wasn't only Faron that had taken on the feminine form.

'Take her up and put her in with Tessa and Gianetta. Bathe her well and give her something decent to wear. Oh, and burn these old rags.'

'You can't treat me like this,' somewhere, Faron is outraged, 'I'm not an object to be pushed here and there.'

'Be a well fed, well looked after object, or be your own person, out on the street. That's the lot of most women, take your choice.'

'Yes Madame,' and Faron found himself doing something that very much resembles an attempt at a curtsey.

'Come,' the older woman scoops her up, and directs her up the long, winding, golden staircase.

'In just seven days …?

' … I can make you a woman.'

10. Virgin territory

'Come, this will be your room', she leads him into a large bed chamber with three Victorian type beds against the three facing walls. The rest of the furniture is fairly modern, inexpensive and slightly used.

'Is it really you?'

'Don't you ever get bored of asking that same stupid question? Who else can I be but myself''

'What, what has happened? How can you be an old woman? How can I be Aideen? I don't understand any of this.'

'What is there to understand? You wished to understand what it is like to be on the other side of the equation, so here you are.'

'But I cannot be Aideen, I cannot be my own daughter.'

'Fine, then you aren't.'

'Don't mock me, you know what I mean. Can you turn me into anything at any time?'

'No, not at any time, only when it's funny. You can be anyone or anything, just as long as it helps you to understand yourself better.'

'And what will understanding bring to me? I suppose that you can't know, but I spent quite a lot of time with all sorts of shrinks, and lots of alternative shit as well.'

'And did it do you any good?'

'Maybe a bit, but not where it counted. I came out of all that much the same loser that I was before I started.'

'So all those forms of therapy failed to touch the roots of your problems?'

'Nothing can sort out my problems.'

'Well let's not hope that your right.'

'Because?'

'Because we'll be spending a hell of a lot of time together otherwise.'

'Meaning?'

'That until you succeed to sort out your stuff, ebony and ivory, we'll be together forever.'

'You say, until I succeed, that would suggest that you think that it is possible that someday I'll sort all my stuff out.'

'Maybe not all your stuff, as you put it, but certainly the most of it.'

'And my living as Aideen is part of that process?'

'It would seem so.'

'You don't know?'

'How should I know? I'm not God. Just look at me, do I look like God?'

Suddenly Faron sees the ridiculousness of this situation and breaks into uncontrollable fits of laughter. He is still laughing as two women of the establishment enter.

One is tall, she carries herself in a quiet, self-assured manner. It comes as no great surprise when Faron realises that it is no other than Helen, his brother's wife, daughter of a Harley street physician.

The other woman, smaller, much quieter, self-effacing is much more difficult to place, however, she does remind him of someone, but just who and where, doesn't register immediately.

Actually, to be strictly honest, none of this enters into his conscious mind of the moment, he is still overcome by the idea that the fat, wheezy, spinster, planted in front of him like an ugly, female version of Timothy the Toad, is in fact God!

'Are you alright?' Helen runs over to him showing real signs of concern.

'Sorry, yes, yes, I'm fine, it's just, just, just ,' and again he breaks down into uncontrollable fits of laughing and squeaking. 'She, she, her, it's just, God, how could you be God?'

Now it is Guida's turn, she becomes redder and redder, and she starts to giggle, a weird, mouse like, high pitched giggle.'

'Yes, yes, don't you see, that's it, I'm God, I hadn't realised it before. Of course, I must be God, just look at me, it's totally obvious.'

Laughter, like yawning has that miraculous possibility to infect others in close proximity, and before many more minutes have passed, both the new arrivals have started to catch the giggles.

'Are you supposed to be God, Guida?' Helen is making as if to take a photograph of the old woman, framing the image through a gap between her hands.

'I bow before you, oh great one,' as the other bows, Faron catches the movement and links it to a distant memory, Indonesia.

This girl is one of the workers in the Batik factory. How and why she should be here, to appear in this, weirdest of experiences, is a question that he would ponder, later, in a quieter moment.

'Guida!' The command comes from somewhere outside of their room, and from the tone, it is not to be ignored.

'I am so sorry, but it seems that God is required for other divine duties, I must leave you.' Stifling her laughter, she drops slightly towards the ground, being the best she can offer as a curtsey, and wheezes off.

The exit of Guida, breaks the spell and the laughter fades gently away.

'Hello,' smiles Helen, 'my name is Tessa.'

'And I'm Gianetta,' she gives a little curtsey in Faron's direction.

'Hi, I'm, I'm Aideen, I'm new here.'

'We might have noticed,' Helen / Tessa, it is still she that commands, that speaks first, that directs the conversations. 'So you are signora Mallevaichi's new protégé'.

'Who?'

'Nicola Mallevaichi, the 'Signora' for whom we all work.'

'So you are, all, you are …?'

'Actually no, we are not all prostitutes. Most of them are, but we are not, we are just hostesses.'

'That is why you have been placed in this room with us,' she adds shyly.

What is she doing in my fantasy, why is she here? The question troubles Faron, at the same time trying to integrate all this new information.

'The other girls call this, 'virgin territory', because we are possibly the only legal aged virgins left in Venice.'

He is warming up to her, it is if he had never had a conversation with her before, but then again, when would have had anything to say to the wife of his estranged, younger brother?

'I suppose I am very much a virgin to all this.'

'Don't worry, we're now here to look after you.'

Such openness and friendliness comes as something of a surprise to Faron, he had ceased to see these girls as little more than pleasure objects. As if the human being had been excluded from the equation.

'What does that mean?' He gives a little, slightly nervous smile.

'Looking at you, it seems that you have missed out on some of the basic education of just what it means to be a woman.'

You're telling me. 'I hope that it's not going to hurt.'

'Not too much, we'll do our best.'

'Don't be silly, Gianetta, of course it's going to hurt. Being beautiful is a very painful business.' She is laughing and smiling as she mocks Faron, he allows her to take is arm, but not without some trepidation.

There is a slight tapping on the door.

'What is it, Guida?'

'Signora wishes for Aideen to wear these, and you are all to dine with her this evening. Eight o'clock, do not be late.'

'As if we would dare.'

'Why are we to dine with la Signora?' Gianetta seemed quite nervous.

'When signora Mallevaichi chooses to confide in me her secrets and schemes, I will be better placed to share them with you. Until then, you might ask her, if you should so wish.' She places the pretty dress on Aideen's bed, makes a gesture of a curtsey and leaves.

'So, let the torture begin.'

'It sounds that you are looking forward to this.'

'We all take our little pleasures, where we might. Now, off with those ugly rags, we mice have only a few hours to prepare you for your first public appearance.'

'It won't hurt too much,' sweet Gianetta, still trying to reassure him, but now, not so successfully.

'Oh my God, your legs, have you been crossed with a monkey or something?'

'Tessa, don't be so mean.'

'Wax or epilator?'

'What?'

'You get to choose your own torture instrument, wax or epilator?'

'What's the difference?' Of course he is not totally unaware that women do not have silky smooth, hairless legs naturally, but the intimate details of such, he has never bothered to acquaint himself with.

'This is going to be educative for you. Waxing is simple, we heat up strips of wax coated material until the wax becomes sticky, we wrap them around your legs, in a few seconds, the burning stops and the hairs stick to the wax, and then we rip them off, and you try not to scream too loud, so not to disturb the other girls who often sleep during the day.'

'That's what I seem to have heard.'

'Want to try?' She seems quite motivated.

'And the other thing?'

'Epilating takes a little longer, but it hurts a bit less, and you soon get used to it,' Gianetta was still trying to protect him.

'So why don't we try that then?'

'It takes quite a long time, and it's a bit boring.'

'Because I'm not going to be screaming in pain every few seconds?'

'You see, you're getting to know me, already. Gi, she can have my old epilator, I bought a new one last week.'

'What was wrong with the old one?'

'Don't worry, it still works, I change mine every few months, the newer they are, the faster they get the job done.'

Gianetta brings the pink object, not so different than a normal electric razor. It is only on looking closer that one notices that there are no horizontal, circular blades, but a pair of rollers across and leading into the inside of the machine, like an old clothes mangle, for those old enough to know what that object looks like.

'Okay, bring that chair into the bathroom, here we can suck out all the air, so no-one can hear you scream.'

'I thought that it was the waxing that was painful?'

'The waxing is more painful and quicker. Epilating is *slightly* less painful but takes much, much longer.'

'Sort of between the rock and the hard stuff.'

'Sort of, ready?'

'Bring it on. Awww!'

'What's wrong, are you all right?'

'Of course she is, it just takes some getting used to, don't you remember the first time that you epilated?'

'It was quite a long time ago.'

'And so it should have been for you, my little monkey. Can you try to be a little more dignified, after all, we are women, we know about pain.'

'And what do you mean by that?'

'Men don't know anything. See how he would cope having a period once every month. And if it were men that gave birth, the human species would never have survived. Men go to wars, get into fights, but accepting pain, repeated and intense pain, they don't know they've been born.'

'Okay, if that's what you think, then I'm ready, I'll just sing my Indian torture song.'

'That's my gal,' and she switches the innocent, pink toy onto high and restarts to caress Faron's hairy legs.

'Hey, you've already done that bit.'

'Do you think that just one pass is enough to get rid of all this forest?'

'It's worse than cutting a lawn with an old, rusty, manual lawn mower.'

'Of course it is, we need to remove every blade of grass.'

'Hey, how high do you think that you're going with that thing?'

'We need to clean your bikini line, you can trim yourself when you take your bath. I suppose that you're not the 'clean shaven' type.' Faron of course understands the reference.

'No, I am certainly not into shaving down there.'

'Well, I certainly hope that you'll give it a good trim. Having fanny hairs sticking out is not acceptable here.'

'Shaving? Couldn't I just shave my legs?' The idea suddenly became obvious and very attractive.

'Sure, it's just that you need to shave them every day and most of us would rather something that lasts a little longer.'

'Gi, you shave your pussy, do you have a spare for Aideen?'

'Of course, here you are.' She hands him a body razor after replacing the head.

'Now, what to do with your arms, shave or bleach?'

'Bleach is more elegant and shaving your legs and your arms each day will take a very long time.'

'Gi's right, bleach it is.'

'Bleach? Is it safe?' Something that Faron wasn't aware of.

' 'Course it is, silly, look, I use it all the time,' she shows him her thin, dark skinned arm, the gold, white strands of hair float slightly with the movement.

'If you're going to shave, get into the tub and do that now, when you're done, give us a call and we'll see to the beach and a mask.'

'A mask?'

'Sure, haven't you seen just how ugly you are?'

'Tessa, you are so mean!'

'You're skin looks like you could sand wood with it. Crocodiles have smoother complexions than you do. But don't worry, a good peeling should take off a nice few layers and we might just discover something a little bit softer.'

Under all these insults, Faron could still feel the caring and support of before. So he takes it all in good stead, reached out for the razor and can of foam and stands in the bath.

'You know, we are all girls, you don't have to bath in your knickers. Wait a minute, you weren't a nun in another life? Hairy legs, hiding your tush, it all adds up.'

'No, I wasn't a nun.'

'Just a thought, call us when you're done.'

Faron isn't so much shy about revealing himself to the two girls, it is much more complicated than that. You see, he has inherited the body of his own daughter, there is a very normal and natural taboo about seeing your own sexually mature daughter naked.

By looking at this body, he is indeed crossing that taboo, and that is making him very uncomfortable. However, at the end of the day, he has to bathe, and at some time he will have to go to the toilet and so he will just have to deal with it.

He sighs, and twists his arms behind his back to open his bra.

As someone that has opened literally hundreds of bras, even eventually with only one hand, opening the four little hooks prove to be surprisingly difficult.
Eventually he gives up the more elegant technique, slips his arms from out of the straps and pulls the band round and down. With the hooks in front of him and at the level of his naval, he succeeds without further t'do.

Taking off his slip has no technical difficulty attached, only the aforementioned resistance, sighing a second time he pulls the garment off and down. What strikes him as weird is the size of his posterior.

Aideen is slim of build, but taking the underwear off, Faron is made aware that even if thin, women have bottoms that round out, and he has to manoeuvre the shorts more from the back, to get them off.

The actual act of shaving his legs provides no particular difficulty other than a certain attention behind the knees, the inner parts of his thighs and deciding just how high to go around his back-side. It is after that, while picking up the manicure scissors to trim his pubic hairs that he again becomes concerned.

Knowing just how painful it can be to have once trapped the end of his penis in the zip of his pants, he is rather concerned with the sensitivity of his newly discovered genitalia and what would happen if he accidently cuts himself.

I'll just have to be very careful now, won't I? And so he sets himself to the task in hand. At the end, it didn't prove to be anything like as difficult as he had feared.

He just trimmed the hairs to about half an inch all over, and that centimetre and a bit was quite sufficient as a length to keep the scissors far enough away from his sensitive bits, to not cause any worries.

'Okay, I'm done with that, what's next?'

The girls come rushing in, Tessa grabs for his legs.

'What the…?'

'Just checking, not bad, smooth, smooth, good job.'

'Thanks a lot?'

'She was just checking if you missed a bit.'

'No I was not, I taking the opportunity to have a feely of her legs.'

'Do they pass muster, then?'

'I said that they were okay, just remember, every morning, just as smooth.'

'Is she always as tough as that?'

'If you think that I'm tough, just wait until the Signora gets through with you.'

'Can we talk about something else?' Faron is not used to these feelings of discomfort flooding his new body. He knows about fear, about physical, emotional and financial dangers; to be physically hurt, abused and abandoned, to be ruined, but never to be really scared of someone because they intimidated him.

This is a really weird and strange sensation, *I am afraid of this bitch because she can be angry with me, how ...?*

'You're totally right, now is the good part. Out of the bath, do you want a towel?' He had totally zapped being naked, and it didn't seem at all to matter.

'No, thanks, I'm fine, it's quite warm in here.'

'Yeh, there's really good heating in here, not all buildings in Venice have such good heating, she also sees to things like that.'

'Okay, into the bubbles', now that was more like it. Faron wasted no time slipping into the warm scented water.

'Would you like me to wash your hair, Aideen?'

'Yes, please Gianetta that would be very nice of you', she really was a nice person.

And so, for the first time that day, Faron started to relax. Yes there would be more weird stuff to face, being a young woman will surely bring with it many discomforts and discoveries, but this moment, in the warm, scented bath, in a beautiful gilded bathroom, Gianetta gently washing his hair and Tessa preparing some bizarre concoction to slap all over his face, this was a moment to savour, a moment of pure pleasure.

11. Gilding the lilies

'I don't suppose that you're an expert on putting on makeup?'

Faron just looks sheepishly at Tessa and shrugs his narrow shoulders.

'Come on, I'll just do something basic. Oh my God, your eyebrows! Have you never …? Well of course not, when would you have been having them plucked? I suppose that it's a bit late now, I'll just have to add more shadow and mascara.'

'Couldn't you just add a thicker layer of foundation and cover them up?'

'Do you want to do it?' She sounded a little vexed with Gianetta, 'do you know how awful that can look?'

'It was just an idea', she sounded a little upset.

'Thanks for the idea, anyway', Faron tried to soften the blow.

'Sure, it was worth sharing', *thanks Tessa, thanks for being a human being.*

'You have a wonderful colour hair.'

'Yes, it comes from my mother's side, she's Irish and she's got the most incredible green eyes.' It just came out, so natural, so friendly.

Faron, for all his years on earth had never really succeeded to be relaxed and natural with members of the opposite sex. Not that they were the opposite sex now, but they were still women, and he was comfortable to hang out and chat with them.

'Red hair and green eyes, how wonderful. It didn't make you feel jealous not to have your mother's green eyes.'

'Gianetta, that's none of our business.'

'Oh I'm sorry, did I speak out of turn?'

'No, not at all. It's a very valid question. I have the brown, almond shaped eyes of my father and grandmother.

I'm very proud to have the same eyes as them, that way I can always remember that I am part of their family.' And for no apparent reason, Faron's eyes well up, and he starts to gently cry.

'Are you okay?'

'Okay or not, you'd better stop crying soon, I have your eyes to do. And I'm not having you wreck my work, even before I've started.'

'Tessa, don't be mean.'

'It's okay, I don't know where that came from, honestly I don't.'

'Do you need another tissue?'

'Thanks Gianetta, I think that it's passed now.'

'Is it safe to start with your eyes now?'

'Sure.'

'I need you to look up.'

'Hey! What are you doing?'

'I'm blacking your tear line, honey.'

'It looks like you want to stick that pencil in my eye.'

'Trust me, it will look okay.'

'Can't we just do something simple tonight, and you can carry on the torture tomorrow?'

'If you don't look dressed and made up correctly, she will just send us back up here to finish the job and we will have made her angry.'

'And She-who-must-be-obeyed must not be made angry,' but before he had even finished uttering the words, he knew full well that he would NEVER intentionally upset her either. Maybe Faron was not afraid of any woman, but Aideen was petrified of her.

'Okay, but please be careful.'

'I'll be careful', and of course she was. Faron quietly allowed himself to be made up.

For some reason he really enjoyed watching the effect of the mascara pumping up his pale ginger lashes, almost as much as the magical effect of the blusher, as it seemed to sharpen and narrow his face with just a few strokes of the deep rose magical, fairy dust.

Faith, trust and blusher, and I can fly.

The dress was quite simple, turquoise with white edgings, sleeveless but with wide shoulder straps, a modest décolleté, gathered at the waist, but not tightly so, the lower part was cut in an A line, finishing just above knee.

The ensemble was finished with a pair of simple strap sandals, with almost no heel.

In short, for someone who had never worn woman's clothes before, it was a particularly easy entry into the experience. If only that wasn't about to change.

12. The Devil eats Pasta

They descend the golden staircase three in a line, Gianetta, Tessa and Aideen benefitting from the highly polished handrail. It isn't that difficult to walk in the sandals, they fit well enough and the low heels don't prove much of a hindrance.

It was just that holding onto the rail provides an additional support that his female side is needing at this time.

Madame, appears, smiling, beautifully and elegantly gowned and made up as usual.

'Why, my dear you have cleaned up very well. And I'm sure that she has benefitted from both your help and support, well done.' And while, as if gently stroking a random lock of hair from her eyebrow, she looks directly at Tessa. 'Although perfection takes a little longer.'

Tessa looks a little uncomfortable, 'there are still details to be looked after.'

'Good, tomorrow.' She smiles again, Tessa smiles back, they are led to the table and take their seats.

Never smile at a crocodile, Faron reminds himself.

The table is set for several courses, with three sets of knives and forks. Faron again feels the panic welling up from inside, his heart is beating faster, his breath becomes quicker and increasingly shallow, even his hand is beginning to shake.

I need to get out of here, I need to get out now.

'Are you feeling unwell?'

'I just need a moment of fresh air, if you would please excuse me.' He gets up, careful not to bang into the table and knock over the elaborate setting.

'I'll just be a moment.' He rushes, as slowly as possible towards the front door. Before he can reach to open it, someone else arrives and opens it for him. Not looking to see who it is, he continues until he is out of the building.

'Would a cigarette help?'

'Thank you, oh it's you.'

'Who else would it be?' The same game, this time particularly reassuring.

The now elegant young woman and the still inelegant old maid squat down for a calming smoke.

'What happened?'

'I, I, I panicked. It must have been because of the table.'

'Scary things, tables.'

'Please don't make fun of me. This me, Aideen, gets frightened, I, she, FUCK I don't even know how to talk right. I am feeling huge waves of fear, I don't know how to handle this. I panicked because of all the place settings, I'm scared that I don't know how to eat like that.'

'But do you know how to eat at a formal dinner?'

'Well of course I do, but Aideen …'

'… is also you. Just remember that you are also Faron, you can help calm the scared Aideen, you know very well how to behave yourself in company.'

'If nothing else, my mother taught me that.'

'So, go have dinner with your mother, it is almost exactly the same.'

'You're quite right, thanks for the advice, and for the smoke,' And with that Faron gets up and re-enters the house. He is feeling fairly confident and cheerful as he enters the dining room. He is quickly struck by an icy wave of silence. As he approaches the table, he also notices that no-one is moving.

Suddenly he is noticed, 'I trust that you are feeling a little better, maybe you both would like to go outside and fill your lungs with disgusting smoke.'

She must have already noticed the cigarette odour on him.

'Come, sit down. Unfortunately, I have just discovered some rather disturbing news.'

'Will we have to leave?' Gianetta was almost crying.

'We have a right to our private lives,' Tessa was also scared, but expressed it with defiance.

'Calm down, both of you. No, I will not terminating your activities here, at least not just yet. However, I find it disrespectful of you to have done this without even informing of your intentions.'

'Should I go back to my room?' It would be such a relief not to have stay and eat with this scary dragon women.

'No, please sit, this conversation is nearly concluded. Would you care to name the two culprits?'

'You make them sound like they've done something wrong.'

'Gianetta, I just would like to know the names of the two gentlemen that have married two of my young ladies, without even the civility to inform me of their intentions.'

'Giuseppe.'

'Gianetta?'

'Luiz.'

'The minstrels?'

'They call their group 'The River Men'.

'Thank you, Tessa. So you have both chosen to marry those penniless musicians, when I could have introduced you to some of the noblest and richest men in all of Venice?'

'We love them.'

'Fine, let us forget this unpleasant conversation for now, let us eat.'

The meal then passed in an unexpectedly pleasant fashion, Maman, as Faron continued to think of her, when Aideen was not contaminating his mind with waves of fear and anguish, still knew how to carry a full evenings' conversation, pretty much on her own.

She was full of the most wonderful gossip of most of the noble houses of Venice, who was doing what and to whom.

The other reason why things rolled so well was that Faron had succeeded to calm his nerves and to remember all that he had had drilled into him over innumerable Friday night dinners with his parents, especially this impressive looking woman, lording over the head of the table.

His impeccable table manners must have been a very unexpected and pleasant surprise for her, and it put her in an unusually agreeable mood. To the point that one might have imagined that she had forgotten all about the unfortunate circumstances, being the weddings.

'Thank you for a most enjoyable meal. Aideen, you have handled yourself with grace and dignity, you can be most proud of yourself.

As for both of you, if you are so proud of your choices that I have to be informed by others, I would suggest that from now on, you risk to display your wedding rings and see what effect it might have on your regular gentlemen callers.'

And with that, she was gone. All that was missing was the swirl of green smoke.

13. A little Gossip, a little Chat

'Please, please, tell me everything.' Faron has no problem allowing Aideen's feminine curiosity to carry him at this time.

'So, why should we tell you anything? We don't even know you, maybe you're a spy for the wicked queen.'

'Don't be so mean, of course we'll tell. We got married', Gianetta squeals in glee.

'So who are the men, are they really musicians, are they famous?'

'No they're not famous, although one day they will be.'

'Are they rich, do they come from noble families?' Has he ever been so totally indiscrete? And yet they don't seem at all put out, in fact they seem to be expecting him to ask.

'No, but it's much more interesting than that.'

'They might be rich, they might be from a rich family.'

'Gianetta, don't get carried away. They are orphans, they are supposed to be brothers, they could even be none identical twins, but nobody knows anything else.'

'But don't you know anything else about them?'

'Not much really, they were brought to Venice as children, by their nurse, who asked Giuseppe if he would be willing to look after them for a while.'

'And then what happened?'

'I'll tell.'

'Okay, you tell if you must.'

'Then something happened to the nurse, she never came back for them. Nobody knows anything else, it's a real mystery.'

'And there's nothing to say who they are?'

'Only this,' Tessa has put on a ring that she had hidden on a string around her neck.

'That's beautiful.'

'It's his.'

'And I have one as well,' Gianetta, shows off her identical ring.

'But they're beautiful, are they gold?'

'Of course not, they'd be worth a fortune if they were.'

'Maybe they are made of real gold.' Tessa shoots her a withering glance.

'But why did you keep it a secret?'

'We were worried that if she were to find out, that she would throw us out into the streets, and this is the only place that we can work and not be forced to sleep with the clientele.'

'We want to stay pure for our boys.' Faron could certainly believe that of Gianetta.

'So what will happen now?'

'Well, we're allowed to stay, but she has insisted that we wear our wedding rings.

If the men refuse to dance with us because we're married, we'll be out of a job anyway.'

'But she can say that she didn't throw us out because we got married', Tessa nods her head.

'That's right, Signora can still appear as a kind supporter of the underprivileged girls of Venice.'

'But what about me?'

'It seems that there was some sort of a bet between her and Colonel Pavoneggiarsi, that she could pass you off at next week's ball as one of us.'

'I bet that you can do it too.'

'Yes, I know, I was there, it was in the square, and again, they discussed it this morning.'

'So how much did they bet?'

'Tessa!'

'It doesn't have to be a secret.'

'Actually, I don't know.'

'Anyway, it can't be much, the Colonel's been broke forever.'

Tap, tap, tap.

'Good night girls, Aideen's get a long day ahead of her'.

'Good night Guida.' The girls quickly get themselves ready for bed.

As long as tomorrow I don't wake up to find myself transformed into a giant cockroach, I suppose that things are not that bad...

14. Breakfast at Tiffany's

The morning finds Faron in good spirits, he has gotten over his discomfort of living in his daughter's body. He is even learning to appreciate the rich emotional tapestry that drives much of her behaviours.

As he can find nothing else, and as Guida has not followed all instructions to the letter, he puts back on the jeans and top and sneakers that he has come in.

'Time for breakfast.'

'Yes, I suppose it is,' Tessa yawns, clearly this is rather early for her to be up. Gianetta seems more of a morning person.

'Come on Aideen, last one down's an old sloth.'

'No running, you two, it'll only get us all into trouble.' *I suppose that the Italians also had their version of the Gestapo.*

'Okay Tessa, we'll be good,' but like two naughty children they skipped and giggled all the way down to the dining room.

Unfortunately that is where Faron's spirits dropped down a notch or two. The breakfast table was as beautifully laid out as the preceding evening. All was shiny gold and sparkling crystal filled with fruit; whole fruits, fruit salad and various fruit juices.

'So where is breakfast?'

'This is breakfast, silly. Who's going to want to dance with a fat hippopotamus? We need to watch our figures.'

'But last night?'

'Last night was exceptional, and didn't you notice that it was only you that ate more than the smallest helpings of everything.'

'Tessa had a large plate of tiramisu.'

'And how long did she stay in the bathroom afterwards?'

'She was taking off her makeup and stuff.'

'And sticking her finger down her throat.'

'I'm sorry, I don't understand.' Gianetta makes the gesture of making herself sick.

'Oh my God, why would she do that?'

'Young lady, you have much to learn about being a woman.'

You're telling me.

'Good morning ladies, have you already finished your breakfasts?'

'We've just arrived, … ma'am,' he quickly adds out of politeness.

'We have only the best coffee, I suggest that you try some, it will help wake you up.'

They are both waiting to see if there is a comment about Aideen's clothing, but it doesn't seem to be troubling the lady of the house.

'It is very good coffee.'

'When you have both finished, you will come to the ballroom. Your clothes and pumps are already in your room, Tessa will also join you. All three can benefit with a session with Master Jacques.'

'Who is Master Jacques?' they were again alone, sipping the coffee and munching on a selection of peeled and diced fruit.

'He is a French dance teacher, I suppose you will be learning to dance for the ball on Saturday.'

'Well, that shouldn't be too bad.'

But it was …

15. The Two-Way Stretch

They reach the bedroom only to find that Tessa has already dressed and left. On their beds they each find a leotard, tights and a pair of dancing pumps.

'They do think of everything.'

'She is very thorough.' Faron certainly had to agree with that.

'Come dancing?'

She gives a deep and low curtsey.

'You'll have to teach me how to do that.'

'Maybe you'll be learning that today.'

'Yes, maybe I will,' and with that, they re-descend the golden staircase and make their way into the grand ballroom.

Master Jacques is the quintessential model of a dance teacher.

Not very tall, nor broad, nor obviously muscular, but as wound and tight as any mechanical mouse that your cat is to be driven crazy with.

He has black, sleeked back hair; black eyes, a black moustache and, just for the artistic licence, one blackened tooth.

'Good morning ladies, I haf been asked to lead you in some warming up exercises.'

'But, aren't you going to teach us some new dances?' Tessa seems to have had expectations.

'No, young lady, today we will be warming up and stretching, especially the legs, in particular, we will be focusing on the calf's.'

'He's already making me think of dinner', Faron was finding Gianetta much more fun than Tessa.

'Dinner is clear soup, with fruit salad for dessert.'

'And the main course?'

'Some of us slip out for a cigarette.'

'So now we start, can we have some music please''

They hadn't noticed but there was someone seated at the piano. Actually, not just any someone, it was Duncan.

'Luiz!' squeaked Gianetta, the excitement running through her like a five hundred bolt electric current.

Now it finally comes clear to Faron.

Duncan, while in Indonesia must have had a relationship with this girl. And even if he, Faron, had not consciously realised it, it must have been registered somewhere in his unconscious. And now, in this dream created reality, here they both were, together, married.

But what had stopped them marrying in real life? Maybe they did marry, but more than likely, his selling off the business and stabbing Duncan in the back, wouldn't have helped that situation.

Well, at least, now here, they are married and nothing is likely to spoil that.

'First we do ankle circles, left foot, to the left. If you cannot balance on your right foot, please find a chair to lean on.' He felt slightly embarrassed that he didn't have the same balance as the other two, but that was that, he went and got himself a chair.

'Now to the right.' Then there is the right foot. From there they do something from the Ministry of Silly Walks, something that Groucho would do, bending their knees and walking close to the ground. Then walking on tip toe, before walking, leaning as far forward as possible.

Then there were all types of stretches, against the wall, using their hands, and then elbows to balance themselves.

Touching their toes, standing, sitting, crouching backwards. And on and on.

They were allowed mini breaks, to drink, to pish, but not leave for a smoke nor any other excuse.

Finally, She entered.

'Is she ready?'

'I think maybe a little massage might still be careful.'

'You are most thorough, I appreciate that.'

'Says one perfectionist to another', Faron and Gianetta both smile at her reflection.

'Come, Tessa and Gianetta, here is some oil, and fresh towels, you are to massage the new girls calves for ten minutes. It is important that they are well warmed and supple.' And then they leave the girls to it.

'What is all this for?'

'I really don't know, I ..., Gi, could you please concentrate. Even if we have no idea why we are doing this, it must be important.'

'Thank you girls, you seem to have done a good job. Now Aideen sit yourself down on that chair and put these on.' A girl arrives from somewhere carrying a pair of stilettos that must have been at least six if not eight inches high. Whether that converted to 15 or 20 centimetres, was almost irrelevant, Faron is both speechless and motionless with shock.

'Here, let me.'

'Thank you, Gianetta. At least someone hasn't fallen totally into some magical, hypnotic spell.

The little girl takes a shoe and kneels down in front of Faron, slips off the dance slipper and slides his foot into the stilt like object.

If it fits I wonder if I'll be whisked away to some castle somewhere and end up marrying a prince, who might or might not be the principal from my old boarding school.

'There, thank you Gianetta. Now, you must get up very gently, you can lean a little on your friends for support.' Faron slowly and carefully pulls himself up to his feet. At first the massive heels block his getting up, but he then slides himself over onto his toes, and bending his knees forwards, he manages to get to his feet.

His two new girlfriends help him steady himself.

'From now on, these will be your only footwear, you wear them at all times, but before you put them on, you must spend fifteen minutes warming up your calf muscles with exercise and massage. Is that clear?'

'Yes, yes, ma'am.'

'Now, we have ten minutes left before lunch, help her to walk around a little. Don't worry yet about style, we'll get to that a little later. I'll see you all in the dining room.'

'Is she serious?'

'Have you ever seen her being anything else? Gi, will you concentrate, you nearly let her drop.'

'Oh, I'm so sorry, Aideen, I was a little distracted.'

'It's okay, Tessa, do you think that we can manage just the two of us?'

'If you fall down, then it's you that suffers.'

'Let's risk it then. Go to him. You know that lovers are the luckiest people in the world?'

'Only when they're together.' *This Tessa, Helen, I could really grow to like her. I see now what Jay sees in her. Jay! Could her Giuseppe, be Jay?*

'Careful, you nearly fell down.'

'Sorry, I was just thinking of something.'

'Better just think about not falling down, you can really hurt your ankles if you fall.'

'Spoken like someone that knows what she's talking about.'

'We all fall down from time to time, if you do, don't forget to bend your legs and try to fall on your knees, even if they look ugly for a while, it's less bad than breaking an ankle.'

'So much to learn.'

'And so little to eat, come it must be lunch time.'

'Aideen, you are lean on that stool and keep your feet on the floor at all times.' She has returned without either of them noticing.

'Is this meant to be some sort of torture?' She whispers to Tessa.

'It's something to do with your wearing heels for the first time, but I'm not exactly sure what the point is.'

'Tessa, would you be kind enough to serve your friend, she's not able to serve herself. Where has Gianetta gotten to?'

'She had an errand to run, she'll be back soon. I can look after Aideen, no problem.'

The little crisis passes and lunch, for what it is, is pleasant enough. The experience of wearing the shoes is actually quite amusing, rocking a little forwards then backwards. Just as long as he wasn't being asked to stand up, let alone walk in these dangerous objects.

16. Brush up your Shakespeare

'Come, it is time for Cinderella to start to work for her keep. Tessa and, oh good, you've bothered to grace us with your presence Gianetta, you will assist Aideen into the court yard, she has work to do out there.'

'How am supposed to work, I can hardly stand up alone, never mind do anything useful.'

'Shush, she might hear you,'

'Thank you Gianetta, I have perfectly good hearing. And as for what I have planned for you, young lady, you will listen attentively to my instructions and follow them all out, word for word. That way you will progress satisfactorily.'

The courtyard is a large walled in garden area. Although there are many planted patches, there is also a considerable section that has been tiled over. The combined winds and rain of the past few days have caused piles of leaves to be blown off of the surrounding trees, which are now littering the tiles.

'Here,' she gives Faron a stiff hearth broom made in the old fashioned style using broomcorn.

Faron is reflecting on the choice to keep holding onto the arms of the two girls, and feeling physically safe, or risking letting go of one so as to grab hold of the broom, and feeling safe that Maman won't tell him off. Her holding the broom only re-enforces his last night's image of her.

Of course, with her standing there, broom in hand, waiting for him to take it off of her, there is little risk that the unmovable object, (his arm in the arm of Gianetta), is not going to resist the unstoppable object, (the broom coming his way).

'It is quite solid, you can lean on it to keep your balance if necessary. You two may leave, I'm sure that you've better things to do than to hold her up like some ninety year old grandmother.'

The girls show as much reluctance to leave as Faron desires that they stay. But they all know that there ias no choice and the girls abandon Faron to the security of his broom.

'Now listen very closely. You are to sweep up all of the leaves, but not just in any fashion. As you sweep to the right, you advance your right foot at the same time. If you start to lose your balance, you may hold yourself, for a moment using the broom as a support. Then before starting the next sweep, you will catch your balance back onto your feet.

When wearing heels for the first time; remember to keep your knees slightly bent and most of the weight on your toes. What I expect from you this afternoon are only two things; that this courtyard is cleaned and that you haven't fallen over. Is that clear?'

'Yes, ma'am.'

'Good, I'll be back to check up on you later.'

And so Faron begins to sweep up the leaves; brush to the right, step to the right. Brush to the left, step to the left. For the first half hour, he uses the brush to save himself from falling with almost every step.

But soon he begins to get the hang of it, more and more.

He is aware that he must look like some drunken old granny, the way that he is walking, but is gaining increasing satisfaction, with his quickly improving balance.

'I see that you're doing very well. I've brought you out some lemonade, I suppose you must be thirsty by now.'

'Is there somewhere that I could sit, just for a moment?'

'You are not supposed to sit, and for a very good reason.'

'And do you, oh God in old women's clothing, know of this all important reason?'

'I would suggest that you lean against this tree, and stop asking so many questions.'

'Is that the best that you can do? I thought that you were supposed to be some sort of a guide, but you seem as lost as I am. What is all this supposed to be about anyway?'

'You, learning about pleasure.'

'And me, teetering around in death defying doc martins, brushing up last year's dead leaves, this is supposed to teach me about pleasure?'

'Sure is.'

'And just how is this supposed to teach me about pleasure?'

'Sure is a good question. Here, give me back the glass, it must be time for you to get back to work, pleasure is waiting for you.'

Brush right, step right. Brush left, step left. Brush right, step right. Brush left, step left.

The hypnotic power of a simple, repeating, boring stimulus, is well known to all practitioners of this art, (or science, if you insist). And quite soon Faron is lost in, 'do cats eat bats? Do bats eat cats?' And, 'the flagon with the dragon has the pellet with the poison and the pestle with vessel has the brew that is in the chalice from the palace.'

'… Aideen, Aideen, enough! You can stop now, Very good, very good. Did you fall over at all?'

'Not even once.'

'Well done. Now, give me the broom, you don't need it any more. Now, slowly and carefully walk back indoors.'

'But …'

'You don't need it any more, you are perfectly capable to walk without support.'

And, miracle of miracles, it was true. Faron, a little wobbly and unsure of himself at first, soon is walking, slowly and carefully, but alone and unaided back into the big house.

Back into the Ferguson Place.

17. Pluck a little, talk a little

The evening meal is quite fun, the girls are all chatty and relaxed. Being Monday, this is their 'night off', so they can eat slowly, all the time enjoying gossiping about various known men and women of the highest Venetian circles.

Of course 'eating' is a relative term; for them, this is a normal meal, for Faron, this is some sort of evil plot to drive him even more crazy. And worst of it is, it is his two new best friends that are giving him most grief.

'Aideen, what are you thinking of? You cannot take two slices of turkey breast.'

'Tessa's right, Aideen, here, this salad's great.'

However, a certain amount of white wine is available, and having so little food in one's stomach, is exactly what Faron needs to get a slight buzz.

Suddenly, and even without any green smoke, she appears.

'Gianetta, it is about time that someone did something about those overgrown bushes, sticking out of Aideen's forehead. Please can you see to that this evening.'

And without even waiting for the young lady's 'yes ma'am', she has disappeared.

'What is she talking about?'

'Why your eyebrows, silly. She wants me to pluck them for you.'

'Even more pain and suffering?'

'It doesn't really hurt, and Gianetta is really good at it, and very gentle. Come, we first need to get you back up to our room.'

'Can't I just take these things off here?'

'Oh no, she might find out.'

'Gianetta's right, you'd better not. Anyway, I saw you walking in, you're really getting the hang of heels.'

'And you can also lean on the banister.'

'Anyway, going upstairs in heels is really not at all difficult, you just have to step using your toes, your heels don't touch the stairs at all, you'll see.'

And so he does, and with the pleasant surprise that it is as easy as going bare foot.

'You're walking already really well.'

'Gianetta, how long did it take you to get comfortable in heals?'

'Well, no-one starts wearing anything that high. We start with quite small heel, then, little by little we buy higher and higher heels. That way, we get used to it, it's just natural.'

'Then why does she insist that I start with these stilts then?'

'Gianetta's right about getting used to heels gradually, but you are supposed to be presentable by Saturday night, there's just not the time for you to get used to them like everyone else.'

They arrive at their room, Faron rushes, as best he can to his bed, throws himself onto it, and releases himself from his foot fetters.

Tessa is busy pushing the solitary, old easy chair into the centre of the room, just under the dusty chandelier style, electric lights.

Gianetta arrives from their shabby bathroom with a towel and several assorted objects.

'How many of those do you need?'

'She likes to give herself a choice of torture instruments.'

'Don't be mean, Tessa, I need tweezers, an eye brow pencil and sharpener, small scissors and an eye brow brush. Would you like to put your feet up? They must be aching.'

'I guess that you know what you're doing, and yes, a foot stool would be great.'

'Tessa, please.' She throws some clothes off of a decorated box, and brings it over to the chair.

'I'm not here as anyone's servant.'

'Oh, I'm sorry, princess, I thought that is what we were employed to be. Here, Aideen, just make yourself comfortable. Now lay back, and relax, and can close your eyes if you like.'

'I doubt if I will be able to relax with you plucking my hairs out.'

'It's really not that bad, I promise you, and I'll be as gentle as possible.'

'I know you will,' Faron couldn't help himself from replying.

Gianetta starts by placing the length of the eye brow brush along Faron's nose.

'What are you doing?' She makes a mark where the tail joins the eyebrow.

'I'm drawing your eyebrow shape, now look straight at me, good, now the corner of the eye.

Okay, now this side, along the nose, eyes straight please, thank you, and now, there done. That's all you have to do. You can go to sleep now if you want.'

She draws two lines between the dots on both eyes, and then starts to tweezer out the hairs outside of the lines.

'Ow!'

'Sorry, did I hurt you?'

'Aideen, you're a woman, have a little dignity, we know how to suffer to be beautiful.'

'Well I don't.'

'So it's high time that you learnt.'

'Tessa, don't be so mean.'

'You've done my brows for years, and you're the most gentle plucker in the whole of Venice.'

'Are you okay?'

'Sorry, I'm just not used to this, please carry on.' And so she does, in truth it is really not at all that painful and Faron half doses off as the girls continue to chat.

'You know the Giuseppe and Luiz will be playing this Saturday?'

'No Gianetta, how would I possibly know that?'

'Maybe Giuseppe, might have told you.'

'Of course he told me, he's my husband, he's got to tell me everything, anyway they play every night.'

'No, Saturday is going to be a special night, I overheard Colonel Pavoneggiarsi and signora Mallevaichi talking. He's asked her to invite everyone that's anyone in the whole of Venice. Did he tell you that he wasn't really an orphan?'

'Who?'

'Why Luiz, of course.'

'What do you mean? Of course he's an orphan, they both are, that's why we had so much trouble getting married.'

'Luiz told me that he was told that they weren't really orphans, but really the sons of a very rich noble man, that had them sent away to save them from being murdered.'

'Do you believe that?'

'Luiz is my husband, he wouldn't lie to me.'

'And when is his noble father going to find him and restore him to his great wealth?'

'When it's safe.'

'Gianetta, you are so sweet, but sometimes I wonder where your head is. No-one even knows for sure if Luiz and Giuseppe are even really brothers, and there is nothing to prove that came from any family at all.'

'But he said…'

'Owa!'

'Oh I'm sorry, I wasn't concentrating properly, someone is upsetting me.'

'I'm sorry Aideen, I'll leave that conversation for now and allow Gianetta to give you her full attention.'

'There, almost finished. Just have to brush your brows a bit and trim off the stray hairs …. done.'

'Let's see, open your eyes. Not bad, not bad at all. Come Aideen, come into the bathroom, and see the wonders of the eyebrow fairy.'

Faron is half pulled from the chair by his two room-mates and almost thrust into the bathroom.

It is true, Gianetta has done her work and the face of Aideen seems much more open and her eyes, somehow bigger and brighter.

'Yes, yes thank you, you really are the eyebrow fairy.'

And without even a second's hesitation, Faron grabs Gianetta kisses and hugs her.

Gianetta, is pleased with Aideen's reaction.

'It's my pleasure …'

'Good evening ladies. Why Aideen, you look beautiful, well done Gianetta, she will go to ball, after all.'

'Good night Guida.'

'Good night.' And so to bed.

18. Footloose

Faron, not used to going to bed early, finds waking up much less difficult than he remembers from the past. He organises his washing and dressing with the girls, everything seems to flow easily until he goes to get his high heel pumps.

'Do you think that I have to wear these every day?'

'Of course you do, how else will you be comfortable wearing them on Saturday?'

'Tessa's right, you have to wear them every day.'

Resigned to another day in paradise, he bends down to put them on.

'No, not yet!' Tessa ruches over to stop him.

'What now?'

'You can't just put them on like that?'

'Like what?' Faron is totally lost.

'You need to warm up your calves first.'

'I'm not following you.'

'The muscles just above your ankles, are not used to being scrunched up, and wearing heels, scrunches up your muscles.'

'But I wore them all day yesterday, and it was alright.'

'That was because you did stretching exercises before you put them on. And then you kept standing up all day.'

'So today?'

'You need to warm up and stretch your calf muscles before putting them on.'

'Is it really necessary?'

'I think that you should listen to Tessa, she knows about such things.'

'If you're convinced.'

'It's only for your own good.' And so they spend the next ten minutes doing stretching exercises and finally they give Faron a mini massage.

'I think that I could get used to this.'

'You'd better get used to those heels quickly, 'cus I'm not going to doing this for very long. Come let's get down to breakfast and see what your mistress has for you today.'

'You're not very nice, Tessa.'

'At least we know that I'm on your side.'

'And she isn't?'

'Aideen, it's just a bet. She doesn't care for you more than a Wonker bar, she just wants to prove how wonderful she is.'

'But she will make her into a woman, one of us.'

'And then what good will that do for her? To be a hostess for the rest of her days, dancing and maybe bedding the empty headed dukes and counts of our flooded city?'

'Well I'm going to get out of here, Luiz promised me.'

'What, with his millions from his rich, noble family?'

'They are going to be a super, successful band, and earn lots of money, and take us both away from here.'

'Yes, Gianetta, that is the dream, but on this side of the rainbow, dreams don't always come true.

19. Side to side

Faron makes his slow and clumsy descent down the golden stairs and hobbles into the dining room. He helps himself to a bowl of fruit salad and a glass of orange and makes his way over to a bar stool to lean on, thankful that the bar is at a reasonable height to use as a breakfast bar.

'This morning you are to mop the great hall.' Faron is no longer surprised by her sudden appearance, nor by her unreasonable sounding request.

He follows her into the ball room, reminiscing to himself about the first time he entered that room, on the very first night that he appeared in Venice.

Then he was the master of all, now he is obliged to accept and follow the senseless seeming commands of this women, who is also, on some level, his mother.

Does the fact that she is also Maman help him accept her position over him, or does it more elicit a form of teenage type resistance? He will have plenty time to ponder over this reflection while he mops the entire ballroom.

'Please remember, side to side, advancing the foot first, making wide sweeps, and pushing your opposing hip in the opposite direction.'

Faron takes the mop and mimics, what he has understood of the movement.

'No, no, no. You no longer need to lean on the mop, Stand up straight, that's better. Now straighten your legs a little and put you weight evenly on your toes and heels, good. Just allow your posterior to extend more behind you by arching your back a little. Now try again.'

Faron is not at all sure about all the instructions, but does his best, which must have been reasonably correct, because he hears a vague 'hmm, hmm', turns round and again finds himself alone.

'Disappeared back to the warehouse, have we?' He amuses himself with the image.

Okay Grasshopper, today it's side to side.

And so he begins to mop the old, marble, gold streaked floor. What he finds odd, even surprising, that he is able to recreate the desired movement, without that much effort, and he is steadier and steadier on his feet.

He starts to experiment with lifting his foot a distance off of floor before placing it back down before the sweep of the mop. He wobbles a bit to begin with, but quite soon he is able to balance, comfortably on one foot, for several seconds, without problem.

'Not bad, not bad at all, she'll make a ballerina of you yet.'

Faron loses his balance and almost falls down, he hadn't noticed anyone coming in.

'Here,' strong arms appear out of nowhere, and grab Faron, catching and steadying him until he regains his balance.

'Sorry, I didn't mean to startle you.'

'Thank you Mike, sorry, Marco. It's alright, you can let go of me now.'

Marco seems to have forgotten to release Faron.

'Oh, sorry,' he turns a little red, slightly embarrassed.

'I hope that nobody saw use.'

'Is touching me such an awful thing?' Faron finds himself feeling excited, shy and slightly hurt, all at the same time.

'It's just that I wouldn't want her to think that I was being too friendly with someone else.'

'And just who might she be?' Hurt, jealous and inquisitive, Faron feels as though he is looking onto a scene that he not really participating in.

'I, I, can't say.'

'Why not''

'Because, because it's a secret.'

'Have you also married someone in secret?'

'I wish, but we can never be married.'

'Is she already married then?' Feelings of hope and renewed excitement run through Faron's lithe, little body.

'She's betrothed.'

'Like engaged?'

'It's more than being engaged, it's a legal contract.'

'Then why not just give her up? There are many other women around, you just have to open your eyes, and you'll see.' *Like the one standing here right in front of you.*

Faron is both fascinated and equally appalled with the idea that Aideen, which is himself, is actually interested emotionally and, good God, sexually in Mike.

'But we love each other.'

'If she loves you so much, how come that she's gotten herself, **betrothed** to someone else then?' There's a killer argument for you.

'She was betrothed as a child, and she has no say in the matter.'

'Oh yes? Is he handsome, is he rich? Answer the second question first.'

'Yes he is rich, but we don't know if he's handsome.'

'What, does he wear a mask or something?'

'No, nothing like that. We don't know if he's handsome or not, as we've never seen him.'

'What do you mean, you've never seen him?'

'Quite soon after they were betrothed, as a young child, he was taken into hiding as there was a threat of an uprising against his family.'

'What, did they own the local factory?' Faron fantasies an uprising against his father.

'He is a Duke from a rich and noble house.'

'Wow, good catch for her.'

'She doesn't want to marry anyone else, but her father, who is also from a good family, but rather poor, insists that she marries the Duke.'

'So he knows who he is then?'

'No, only that the boy was brought here, to Venice, and that the family have left some sort of sign so that he can be recognised with.'

'But no-one knows what that is?'

'No-one.'

'Anyway, if she is betrothed, then you might as well give her up.'

'Never, if I cannot have her, I will never take another women ever.'

'Not ever,' he stops for a moment a pulls out an ornate pocket watch, 'oh my ears and whiskers, I'm late.' And with that, he rushes out of the hall.

Never take another woman? Well, we'll see about that, won't we? Faron has the impression that he is ears-dropping on someone else's conversation.

The idea that he, Faron, could find himself making love to Mike fills him with both apprehension and disgust. To rid himself of these all invading and undeniably unpleasant images, he doubles his efforts cleaning the floor, and mops his way through to the end of the morning.

20. Gazpacho and gossip

Lunch is rather uneventful and uninteresting. The food is of the best quality, but sparse and not very appetising. Faron is used to eating much, much more and much, much less healthily.

He is also more than a little preoccupied by his female part's attraction to Mike, and is concerned to realise that there are moments when he totally loses all control of this body. 'She' is capable to say and do anything, and 'he' is totally incapable to stop her in any way.

Up until this morning, it had only been the odd remark, but now he is aware just how much she still exists in this body, and when she wants something, just how much she is able to express herself to get it.

'Thousand lira for your thoughts.'

'Sorry Gianetta, I was miles away.'

'Are you okay?'

'Marco, ' *oh God, what is she going to say now?* 'Do you know anything about him?'

'Not much really, he works for Colonel Pavoneggiarsi, it seems that he has been part of his household forever, I suppose that his mother worked for him too. Why do want to know?'

'Do you think that he's cute?' *Oh God, oh God. What have I done to deserve this?*

'Yes, and strong looking.'

'And totally unavailable.'

'Tessa, how could you?'

'How could I what?'

'How could you think to say that he's totally unavailable?'

'Because he's in love with some bitch.'

'Aideen, you know as well?'

'She knows what? What do you both know that I don't?' Gianetta is almost crying with frustration.

'That Marco is in love with Casilda.'

'Who's Casilda?' Now it is Aideen that lacks information.

'I thought that you knew.'

'This is just not fair. Marco is in love with Casilda, and both of you knew, and no one thought to share that very, very juicy bit of gossip with me? And I thought that we were friends.'

'Sorry, Gianetta, I thought that everyone knew. Just watch them when they're together, and if you check, you'll see that often they both disappear at the same time.'

'Well I never saw any of that.'

'So who is this Casilda?' *You don't give up easily, do you bitch? Somewhere in my youth or childhood I must have done something bad. Well, really, I suppose I did.*

'Casilda is the daughter of Colonel Pavoneggiarsi.'

'Who is the employer of Marco?'

'Yes,' Tessa confirms and continues, 'the two have grown up together, but because Marco is only a servant, they've never really been able to be together.'

'But enough to fall in love?'

'Yes Gianetta, a certain frustration can be a very important element in building desire.'

'So do you think that they'll get married?'

The other girls stop for a split second, before replying in unison. 'They can't.'

'They can't?'

'Who can't what?' Again, out of nowhere

'They, they can't help me to prepare myself for Saturday night's ball, because they don't know what your plans are, ma'am.' *That was well done, she's at least learnt something from her old man.*

'What they can do is to help you to get into this.' signora Mallevaichi hands Tessa a black object. 'The metal rod goes down the back, just above the posterior. You will meet me back in the ball room, please don't be long.'

21. Up and down

The object that Faron has to succeed to enter into is a tight, elasticated tube that goes from just over the bust line, down to the knees, and with a thin metal rod that runs all the way down the back stopping, just above the bottom.

It takes all three of them a good ten minutes to get Faron into this 'garment'.

'How the hell am I supposed to move in this?'

'Well I think for the New York marathon, a simple track suit might be slightly more appropriate.'

'Tessa, you could be a bit more supportive.'

'More supportive, I'm virtually carrying her downstairs on my own, can't you take a bit more weight. And Aideen, you could make a bit more effort.'

'What, with these stilts and this torture instrument, you think that I can get down these stairs without falling arse over tit?'

'Okay, we're nearly there, just a few more steps, careful Gi, okay, that's got it. Do you think that you can make it into the ballroom alone?'

'Thanks, both of you. I think that Signora would blow a gasket if I came in carried by you two pallbearers.'

'Best of luck.'

'Thanks Gi, thanks Tessa, see you at supper.'

'You still owe us some information.'

'About what?'

'Not what, who?' And laughing, they turn and run off, leaving Faron to risk his entering the grande salle either on all fours or flat on his face.

Take it easy, we can do this. And surprisingly enough, with his back, ramrod straight, head held unusually high, he sails forward into the ballroom.

He is not particularly surprised to find a bucket of soapy water waiting for him, only this time there is no map, only a wash cloth.

'Come here Aideen, your task, this afternoon is wash all the pillars in this room. First you will wash them with this water that has cleaning product in it, then Guida will bring you in soon fresh water to rinse it off with.'

'No problem.'

'Wait, I haven't told you how you should do it yet.'

'It seems pretty obvious.'

'Stupid child. Bend down and pick that cleaning cloth.'

Faron makes to bend as usual, from his waist, legs slightly apart, toes slightly pointing inwards, knees slightly bent. He gets a little less than half way down but the system doesn't work in this situation.

Due to his tight elastic and metal supported 'dress', he cannot spread his legs, nor can he bend his back, not only that, but the heels add an extra couple of inches to his height that makes the cloth even more inaccessible.

'This is impossible.'

'Of course it is, if you try and pick it up that way. Now, put your legs together, that's your feet, knees and thighs. Good. Now, with your weight slightly more on your heels, keep your back straight, slowly bend your knees, and allow gravity to take you down to the cloth.'

Faron does as he is instructed, even though a little unsure, and having to steady himself on the nearby pillar, he succeeds.

'Now take up the cloth, lean slightly more onto your heels, keep your back straight, head looking forward, now just straighten your legs.'

Again, Faron uses the pillar for support, Maman makes no comment on that.

'Be sure to keep your back straight and head looking forward. Now, take the cloth, place it against the pillar, keep your arm straight, use your legs to rub it up and down.'

'Can I use the other arm, or both?'

'As you fancy. What is important is that you look forward and keep your back straight, everything else, do as you wish. I will be checking on you from time to time, but you might not notice my coming or going. Up and down, down and up, just remember head straight forward, back straight up, no bending, only from the knees.'

And … she was gone.

'Down and up, up and down, do cats eat bats? Up and down, up and down, I will lead them up and down. I am feared in field and town. Goblin lead them up and down.'

And so Faron begins his afternoon chores. As with using the brush, he starts by using the pillars as a support and for balance, both going down and also for getting back up.

And, again, after some time, the pillars become unnecessary, he starts to enjoy the movement in itself, he even realises that this tight body stocking is helping him to master these two, simple, but not so obvious movements.

'Ready to rinse?'

'You?'

'Yes, me. Are we to have the conversation about 'am I me', again? Or can we pass on that this time?'

'This body, this being Aideen.'

'Yes?'

'It's not working for me.'

'Is it working against you?'

'That's not funny. Actually, yes, it is working against me.'

'What are you trying to say?'

'I can't control it.'

'Your body.'

'Yes.'

'You seem to be doing well enough at the moment.'

'Yeh, sure, at the moment. But there are other moments, moments when 'she' takes over.'

'What do mean, when 'she' takes over?'

'Don't you know?'

'I don't know what you're talking about.'

'You are so fucking useless. Don't you know that Aideen, my daughter, whose body this is, sometimes just takes over? I'm like some fucking, Pinocchio and she's pulling the fucking strings!'

'Oh, now that's very interesting.'

'You didn't know?'

'Actually, I'm quite new at this.'

'Isn't there some kind of manual for this?'

'I've never seen one.'

'So what are you doing here?'

'I'm here to help you.'

'But you don't know what you're fucking doing.'

'Not all the time.'

'Any of the time?'

'Sure, I have a plan.'

'And what, oh great and glorious wizard, would that plan be?'

'Simple, to accompany you through the seven islands and help you to become the best person that you can be, learn the lessons and so you can continue on your journey.'

'Are there by any chance any more details than that?'

'I have some ideas.'

'Some ideas, is that it, some ideas?'

' 'Fraid so. You can always go back to where we met.'

'That would not be an option.'

'Then just enjoy the ride. You have so much to learn.'

'Like what it would be to be fucked by a man?'

'I doubt that that would happen.'

'I bloody well hope not.'

'Your water's getting cold, and you need to rinse off all the pillars before supper. We have guests tonight and Signora wants to see every golden strand glittering and gleaming.'

'I love thee not, therefore pursue me not. Hence, get thee gone, and follow me no more.'

'Up and down, up and down.'

'Get out you old witch.'

'Parting is such sweet sorrow.'

'Until we meet, upon the morrow.'

And so Faron returns to his pillars, oddly calmed by the interaction with the guide.

His knees and his lower back inform him that they are feeling the effort of this exercise, but he just takes a few deep breaths, shrugs his shoulders and carries on.

22. Dips and dope

'Are you finished yet?' Tessa seems impatient for something.

'Just tidying up. Is something wrong?'

'Of course something's wrong, you left us hanging on like some cheap TV cliff hanger.'

'I promise, I didn't shoot J.R.'

'Are you ready?'

'I suppose that someone will take away the bucket.'

'When they come to finish the cleaning and set up the room, I'm sure that they'll see to that.'

'Finish cleaning? But why did I spend all day mopping the floor and washing the pillars?'

'Beats me, let's go.'

The two then hurry out of the ballroom and into the dining room.

'Wow'.

'What?' Both Aideen and Tessa look inquiringly at Gianetta.

'Have you seen how fast you're walking?'

'What do you mean?' Faron had followed Tessa at her hurried pace, he had not realised that they were both almost running, and he was keeping up with her without any problem.

'Oh my God, I've learned to walk in these things.'

'Come on, let's get ourselves something to eat. I see that someone has not thought to wait for us.' Gianetta blushes slightly.

'Don't let her get to you,' it is now Aideen's turn to support her friend. Faron takes note.

Soon they are sitting at the bar, plates of crudities and a couple of savoury low fat dips to spice them up, have been ferried over to their corner.

'So, tell us why Marco and Casilda can't get married?' Tessa will not wait a moment longer.

'Because Casilda is betrothed.'

'To someone else?' Tessa gives Gianetta a withering look.

'But to who?' Gianetta gives Tessa a sort of withering look back.

'To whom? Not to who.' Tessa smiles gently in Aideen's direction, and shrugs her shoulders.

'Nobody knows.'

'What do you mean, 'nobody knows'?' Tessa hasn't waited all afternoon to be frustrated like this.

'He's some unknown son of a Duke that lives here in Venice.'

'So he's living here incognito.' Gianetta looks a little lost.

'In secret,' Aideen helps out. Faron is experiencing this scene as if he is part of a theatre audience, with a certain amount of amusement and detachment.

'So why is he hiding?' Tessa is not going to give up now.

'Marco says …'

'Marco told you this?' Gianetta is impressed.

'Marco thinks that the young duke was smuggled to Venice to protect him against some sort of revolt against the family.'

'But that must have been years ago, surely things must have sorted themselves out by now.'

'Look Tessa, I only know what he told me. If you're not satisfied with the info that I've got, then go and ask him yourself.'

'I'm sorry Aideen, I didn't mean to be mean. Come on, I'll help you get dressed and made up for tonight, this will be your first appearance in public. I bet that you'll be glad enough to get that monstrosity off of you.'

'What monstrosity?' Faron had completely forgotten that he was wearing the tight black tubing.

'That thing.'

'Oh yes, it's not so bad when you get used to it.'

'I've got some dresses that are not so much more comfortable than that,' Gianetta confined to them as they made their way back up the gilded staircase.

23. The Duke of Burgundy

Aideen, supported and aided by her two friends, dressed and made-up, slowly and carefully descends the ornate staircase.

'I see that you have succeeded to shed your chrysalis and turn yourself into a fairly presentable butterfly.' Faron can feel Aideen's mixed reactions to the Signora's comments, pride and appreciation peppered with anger and resentment. The intensity of the two sets of opposing emotions both scares and fascinates him.

'You are here to watch and observe how the other girls behave. You are not to interact with any of gentlemen, I will see to it that you have an appropriate chaperon.' And then she turns on her elegant heels and flows out into the ballroom to hold court.

'May I?' Faron turns, and almost faints in shock and surprise.

'Marco?'

'The Colonel has graciously loaned me to signora Mallevaichi for this evening, He does that fairly often, I am to be your body guard.'

'I would be honoured if you would be so kind to guard my body tonight. I fear that otherwise I would be in imminent danger.' *Where does she get to talk like that?*

'My pleasure and privilege.' *Why is he seducing her if he is so much in love with Casilda?*

Aideen gives her arm to Marco who gallantly leads her into the ballroom.

Faron is slightly surprised to see Giuseppe and Luiz setting up on the small stage at the far end of the room.

'Oh they play here quite often, they're not bad really.'

'Would you be so kind so as to get me a drink?' *She's still seducing him, the bitch.*

Marco heads off to find themselves a drink as the 'band' starts to play. Luiz is behind the piano, Giuseppe is playing a sort of electric lute.

They both sing:

> The boatmen's our name,
>> But we're not to blame,
>> It's surely a shame
>>> It's not the trade that we ply.
>> For gallantry noted
>> Since we were short-coated,
>> To beauty devoted,
>>> Giuseppe\ Luiz and I
>
> When morning is breaking,
>> Our couches forsaking,
>> To greet their awaking
>>> With carols we come.
>> At summer day's nooning,
>> When weary lagooning,
>> Our mandolins tuning,
>>> We lazily thrum.

Marco returns with the drinks, but before Aideen can even thank him, they are interrupted by the entrance of the Colonel Pavoneggiarsi and his elegant daughter Casilda.

Faron takes a moment to place her, but taking into account Marco's, or should we say Mike's reaction, it doesn't take more than a second or so for Faron to realise that this is in fact Mike's real wife. How does he know this? He has spied on Mike's Facebook page and seen pictures of the two of them, of course there were the wedding photos, amongst others.

The memory of snooping on his Facebook page, instead of accepting the wedding invitation, fills him with a moment of shame and guilt. However, that moment lasts but the merest, fleeting second, because immediately, all the emotional space is filled with a mixture of anger, frustration and jealousy.

Aideen has seen Marco's reaction to the presence of Casilda, and she's experiencing all the usual rage that the proverbial green eyed monster tends to evoke.

'I'll be back in just a few moments,' and he is gone. What type of secret signal codes they have, it is impossible to detect, but almost immediately Casilda has separated herself from her father and has disappeared off into the bustling crowd. No prizes for guessing who she is likely to accidentally bump into.

However, there is no more time to react to this, as the colonel has noticed Faron and is making a beeline for him.

Whatever his intentions were, and what he intended to say to Faron, one will never know. For, as if by magic, just before he gets even the time to wish him good evening, the long shadow of the signora Nicola Mallevaichi cuts between the two.

'Why good evening, Colonel, what a pleasure to see you as always.'

'Signora,' he bows gallantly, 'as beautiful as always.'

'You have come to see how my little protégé is doing?'

'I have merely come to pay my respects to the young lady, and confirm that you are treating her well, as per our agreement.'

'Aideen, are you being well fed and looked after?' Faron can feel the desire to respond in an aggressive way, complaining about being starved and forced to do pointless tasks, but somewhere good sense prevails and Aideen replies.

'I have no complaints as to my treatment here, madame is looking after me in a very caring way and I am learning well how to be a lady.'

'You see, Colonel, everything is as it should be, and on Saturday you will have to concede defeat and pay me our wager.'

'Saturday is only four days away, I'm sure that she's still a long way away from passing herself off as a lady. Now, what's this nonsense of two of your girls getting married?'

'Yes, it is a little irritating, but they are still working as usual. You see, there is Tessa, still one of my most popular girls. '

Tessa notices that she is being talked about, makes her excuses to the man that she is dancing with and comes over to the group. She makes a little curtsey to both Maman and the Colonel.

'Did you wish for something, ma'am?'

'No, I was just reassuring the colonel that even as a newlywed, you are still one of my favourite girls.'

'Please allow me to congratulate you on your marriage,' he takes her hand to kiss it, but stops short.

'What is this?'

'It's my wedding ring, Giuseppe didn't have any money to buy one, so we used this one.'

'Where did he get it from?'

'He didn't steal it, he's always had it. It was tied on a cord to his wrist, he thinks that it might mean something to do with his past.'

'What is it Franco', even Maman was eager to find out.

'This is the royal seal of the Duke of Burgundy, it can only mean one thing.'

'What thing?' It was easy to say that Tessa was starting to panic.

'It means that your husband, what's his name again?'

'Giuseppe.'

'Giuseppe is no other than the lost Duke of Burgundy, heir to all the titles and lands and the betrothed to my daughter Casilda.'

'But, but we're married.'

'I'm afraid not, the contract of marriage between our two families takes precedent over everything else. As of now, I declare that your marriage is illegal and hence is hereby considered as null and void.'

Not surprisingly, Tessa's reaction is to burst violently into tears and to run out of the hall.

'What excellent news.'

Not for Tessa, nor Giuseppe nor Marco nor Casilda. However that does nothing to reduce the growing feelings of excitement and of triumph building in the little body that he is sharing. If Casilda is to marry Giuseppe, then Marco is suddenly very, very available.

24. Then fate o'er-rules,

    that, one man holding troth,
A million fail,
    confounding oath on oath.

They are back in their bedroom, Tessa is sobbing on her bed, she has already beaten it several times, but now the anger has dissipated, and all that remains is sadness and despair.

'It's just not fair, it's just not fair, not fair, not fair.'

Faron finds himself walking over to her bed, sitting down gently, taking her head, placing it on his lap, and stroking her hair.

Softly and gently he starts to sing.

'I saw tomorrow crying, so I stopped to heal her pain,
I heard the wind a-sighing, 'I'll never sing again'.
I felt the day a-breaking, its heart all broken wide,
The rain was crying softly,
    and again the wind, she sighed.

The sleeper sharply wakened, finds this world unreal,
A hundred years of sleep dust,
             has clogged her spinning wheel.
The world cannot be honest, its existence is the lie,
The lie will keep revolving, and the rain will often cry.

I saw tomorrow crying, so I stopped to heal her pain
And heard the wind a-sighing, 'I'll never sing again',

No, it's not fair, but that's the way that it is.'

'But what am I going to do? How can I cope to see him
with her? He's in love with me, we should be together.'

'I don't know, but I'm going to see if I can do
something about it.'

'How, what can you do?'

'I don't know, but I'm going to talk to someone to see
if there's anything that can be done.'

'But who are you going to talk to?'

'Yes, Aideen, who are you planning to talk to?' She had entered unperceived, Faron spun round, faster than a drunk being offered a free beer.

'We need to talk.'

'Why do you want to talk to her? To Guida?'

'Yes,' it suddenly seemed that Gianetta had woken out of some sort of stupor.

'That's between her and me. Came on, let's go find somewhere quiet to talk.'

'You two should be preparing to go to bed.'

'To bed? More like I'm going to Hell,' and she throws herself once more onto her bed, burying her head in the pillow, as if shutting out the light and sound would somehow shut out the pain in her heart.

They stop on one of the stair landings, everyone else is in their rooms.

'So what can I do for you?'

'What is this crap?'

'I don't follow you.'

'This is supposed to teach me about pleasure.'

'That's the idea.'

'Well, so far I've experienced nothing but psychological and physical torture and food deprivation, and the only thing that has made this experience at all copeable have been those two.'

'That's really nice.'

'And now Tessa's had her heart broken because of this stuff of Giuseppe being a Duke, and all.'

'Yes it is rather sad.'

'Fuck you.'

'Pardon?'

'Look, you've created this place, so that I can found pleasure, and the only pleasure I've had is with them, now if she's heart broken, what's that going to do for me?'

'So it's for your personal comfort that you expect me to magically change everything.'

'No, no, not just for me, also for her. She's a sweet girl, caring, generous, giving. She deserves better.'

'You do know that none of this really exists, you haven't forgotten have you?'

'No, I haven't forgotten, but here and now she exists and she is hurting and you can do something about it.'

'What makes you think that?'

'Stop all this screwing around, you created this place.'

'Sorry Faron, but no, I didn't.'

'Then how the fuck does it exist?'

'It is created by you.'

'Okay, if it's created by me, how do I change it?'

'How should I know? I'm only your guide, I'm just here to give you support, support and maybe a little guidance.'

'Then guide me then. Show me how to change this and make Tessa happy again.'

'But do you really want Tessa to have Giuseppe back?'

'Why not?'

'Because if they are back together, then so will Marco and Casilda be together.'

'Oh yes.' A huge feeling of loss and frustration invades Faron's body.

'What is this crap?! How can I have these feelings? How can I be taken over by Aideen? It's just stupid, what type of sick, twisted joke is this? Aideen is my daughter, this is just a weird dream thing. I am me, I cannot also be her and have her thoughts and feelings.'

'Why not?'

'Because I am not her.'

'You have had enough contact with her and other women to have been able to construct the reactions of Aideen.'

'But why do I have to share her body with her?'

'Because, young **woman** that is what you asked for.'

'I know, be careful what you wish for, you just might get it.'

'Good night.'

'Good night.'

25. Wednesday Morning 8 AM

When the three arrive in the dining room, suddenly all conversation stops, and an uncomfortable silence ensues.

'I suppose you all know about me and Giuseppe.'

'We're really sorry,' it was a skinny blonde Anita, who was the first to dare to speak.

She seemed to open some sort of emotional sluice gate, and from there flowed a gushing stream of concern and support. The girls had recreated themselves into some sort of family, and now that one of them was suffering, they all banded together to help.

It was only the discomfort of not knowing how to broach the difficult subject that had kept them from spontaneous expressions of care and sympathy.

How often in life must people wish to help and support another human being, but be permanently blocked, just because they cannot find the key to open the door of connection?

After breakfast they all were invited to a fitness, stretching, dance class, with the brooding Master Jacques, Luiz is already playing something on the piano.

Faron is happy to have a morning without having to wedge himself into his 'heels' and perform some other pointless and mindless menial task.

And, truth be told, he does quite enjoy the class.

'Aideen, you are to wait behind, we have some special exercises for you.'

'Yes, Master Jacques.'

'I am just going out for a drink of water.'

'And a cigarette,' Tessa adds as she leaves.

Faron, having nothing better to do heads over to the piano to watch Luiz tinkering over a new melody. He is about to say something to the pianist when the door is noisily opened.

In walks, or to be exact, stumbles Giuseppe, drunk.

'Good morning my brother, best friend, bastard.'

'Giuseppe, it isn't my fault, please don't take it out on me.'

'You're married to your sweetheart, I'm to be married to that stuck up bitch, from a snob house.'

'Maybe we could all run away.'

'Where? With what? We used up all the little money that we had buying drinks for the weddings.'

'We will get paid on Saturday, we would have some money then.' Giuseppe suddenly starts to laugh, he almost falls down from laughing.

'What's funny?'

'Do you realise how little money we are getting paid for playing here?'

'It's not too bad, in fact it's quite generous.'

'It's peanuts, it's a bagatelle, it's chick feed, it's nothing at all.'

'What are you talking about?'

'I'm talking about being rich. I'm a bloody Duke, I have properties and titles and lands and money.'

'Is that what you want?'

'No, you idiot. What I want is Tessa. Look if you want it, you can have it, sure, aren't you supposed to be my brother?'

'Yes, I suppose so.'

'So you'd be rich, and Gianetta will be a rich bitch and, and Casilda will be a rich bitch and Colonel Pavoneggiarsi will be a rich arsehole. And me, I'll be the richest of you all, and the poorest soul in the whole of humanity.'

'I'm sorry Giuseppe, is there anything that I can do?'

'Sure, you can take my place and marry the bitch, then I could still be married to Tessa.' Suddenly a thought strikes him.

'How old are you?'

'What?'

'How old are you?' This conversation reminds Faron of something from Murder at the Red Barn.

'I don't know, about the same age as you are.'

'You also had a ring, the same as mine.'

'Yes, I gave it Gianetta as a wedding ring, or are you too drunk to remember?'

'You had a ring, the same as mine. You are my brother. You do not know if you are older or younger than me. How do we know that it isn't you that is the oldest, and so it should be you that marries Casilda?'

'Please, please, please Giuseppe, don't tell anyone of this idea. I beg you, for your love for me, please do not tell anyone of this. I would rather die than lose my Gianetta.'

Suddenly they both realise that Faron is standing there and has been all along.

'You, you, you've been listening to us, you are a bad, bad, girl and if you tell anyone about this conversation you'll be beaten with a stick and thrown out into the streets.'

'Signor Giuseppe, whatever your family name is, just 'cus I talk slow, don't mean that I'm stupid.'

'What?'

'Listen, you can't threaten me, I don't threaten easily. Both Gianetta and Tessa are my friends, I wouldn't do anything to hurt either of them, but you must decide what you are going to do about this. Then you will have to tell the girls, they both have a right to know.'

Luiz turns away from Giuseppe and returns to playing the piano. It is the most eloquent argument that he can come up with. For a long moment there is only the sound created by the tiny hammers tapping against the stretched cords of the instrument.

'It's good to be king.'

'I thought that you were a Duke.'

'Yes miss, you're right, but being a king would be better.'

And without a word or a glance towards his blood brother, he straightens himself up and marches from the hall.

Luiz doesn't turn round either, he is too proud to let the young woman see the fine, salty droplets that are escaping his steal grey, blinking eyes.

26. Lunch- Wake

Lunch is a fairly quiet affair, everybody knows,
everyone who has had something to say, has said it.

The rain had fallen
        The love had died,
                The words were spoken
                        And silence replied.

A slice of bread
    A glass of wine,
            A solemn feast
                The dead must dine.

And so they toast
    Departed hope
            Those that remain
                    Must hold and cope

She lifts her glass
    Be of good cheer,
            But clouds the wine
                    With a single tear.

Death becomes her
    Colour and tone
            To walk her path
                To live, alone.

27. Walking the plank

'Tessa, please will you go and get Aideen's shoes for her.' Faron had not spoken to them of the conversation that he had overheard in the morning. He had decided that it wasn't his place and that he was likely to end up someone's enemy, if he did.

Fortunately. Maman had entered and was about to rescue him.

What-ever it is that you want me to do, it'll be okay with me.'

'Aideen, go into the ballroom and warm up your calf muscles. Gianetta, you can go and accompany her, please see that she warms up correctly.'

Faron and Gianetta stroll into the great, gold flecked room and start stretching. The exercises are no different than a ballet warm up, only it is focused uniquely on the lower part of the body. 'Good, here, put your shoes on, young lady, we have work to do.'

Faron smiles wryly to himself, the term 'we' strikes him as amusing, knowing full well that her participation begins and finished with an explanation of the job in hand.

'Ready'.

'Then follow me.'

They head out through a small hallway that Faron has never been through before. The passage turns several times, and finally releases them into a large room. One whole side of the room is taken up with French doors and windows, looking out onto the terrace.

The glass seems weird, as if somehow it is not fixed, but slightly moving, wavering. It is only after a moment or two that he realises that it is not the windows that are shifting, but the reflection of the water. The water being a large swimming pool, which takes most of the floor area of the room.

'Careful, you are not dressed for swimming, and you are not here as a relaxation either.'

Faron takes a step back from the pool and notices the odd presence of a number of wooden beams that cross the width of the pool, of approximately a metre apart.

'What are the wooden things for?' He doesn't have time to think before Aideen asks the question.

'They are to keep you from falling into the water.'

'How is that?'

'Here', she passes Faron a sponge headed mop, 'you are to clean the ceiling above the pool with this.'

'But they are too far apart to walk on, can I push them closer together?'

'They are exactly the distance apart that I wish them to be,' the steel, cold tone means that she is not totally taken by the suggestion.'

'But how am I to cross if they are too far apart to walk on, two at a time?' She holds her with her glittering eye, until Aideen understands. (Faron has again decided to become a 'watcher on the hill' and just observe the interaction between the two women).

'I'm supposed to balance on just the one thingy?'

'I understand that it is called a beam, and yes, you are to clean the ceiling, using this object and traversing the pool, using one beam for each section.'

'But I will fall into the water.'

'If you fall into the water, you will damage that dress and those shoes. For which you will be charged, that charge will be deducted from your room and board privileges.'

Faron can feel the fear and confusion mounting in his little body.

'The privilege that will be equated with the dress and shoes will be that of your supper this evening.'

'Wait,' she had understood, after all. 'Are you saying, that if I fall into the pool, I can't have any supper tonight?'

'You a bright, little one, aren't you?'

'But that's not fair, I need to eat supper, we eat little enough as it is.'

'You have access to a balanced and healthy diet. And if eating supper is that important to you, then that will motivate you, not to fall into the water.'

And, she is gone. Cinderella drops to the floor, mop in hand, sobbing. It is clear for her that there is no way that she will be able to go to the ball.

'Would you like a handkerchief?'

'Go away!' She doesn't even look up to see who the generous soul might be.

'Fine, I was only thinking that I might be able to help.'

'Not unless you have a magic wand that will help me walk across those beam thingies without falling into the water.'

'Sorry, I don't have such a thing.'

'Thought not.'

'But you do.'

'What?' The unexpected response breaks her out of her emotional prison.

She looks up and suddenly her heart begins to race.

'Hello Marco, are you serious about that?'

'Get up and I'll show you.' Faron gets up and Marco takes the mop. He holds it horizontally, like the pole of a tightrope walker.

'By holding the mop like this, it will serve to help your balance. If you use it like this, you can practice walking across the beams until you find your centre. Then you should be able to walk without it, but if you start to wobble, you only need to catch it back like this and you'll get your balance back. Watch.'

He holds the mop in his both hands and starts to walk across one of the beams, it bends slightly in the middle, but Marco seems not to notice and finishes crossing without breaking his stride.

'That was wonderful.'

'Here,' he crosses back to her side, walks behind her, and places the mop into her two open hands. She can feel his warm breath on the nape of her neck. This sends her heart racing and her breath becomes short and staccato.

She accidently, *sure*, loses her balance and falls backwards into him.

'Careful', he catches her, for the second time that week, 'here', and he helps her back onto her feet.

'You will need to be more careful than that, or you'll be sent to bed without any supper.'

'Somebody was listening.'

'Somebody doesn't always have an awful lot to do.'

'Could you help me then?'

'More than my job's worth, I'm sure. No, sorry, no can do. Just take it slow, keep your back straight and your head from looking downwards and you'll do fine. Try fixing your gaze on a point on the other wall, it might help.'

He makes a small wave gesture, smiles slightly and strolls off.

'If you have so little to do, you could have stayed and helped a bit.' She stops and leans on the mop, 'but he didn't have to be spying on me or stop to help me. Marco, you are going to be mine!'

Faron takes Marco's advice and spends a good few minutes crossing and re-crossing the beams, using the mop as a balance pole. Walking across a narrow beam is not the easiest thing in the world, and wearing killer heels does nothing to reduce the level of difficulty.

However, after several days of almost constant wearing and the exercises given, he succeeds particularly well and quite soon he is secure enough to use the pole as a mop and to start cleaning the ceiling.

Soon, he is so focused on getting the ceiling finished, he almost forgets that he is 'walking the plank'. Using the verticals of the windows in one direction and verticals of the decorated tiles which make up the facing wall on the other, he keeps himself directed on the beam.

He has just about reached the half when refreshments arrive.

'You seem to be doing really well.'

'Well, I haven't fallen into the water yet. Do you have any cigarettes, by any chance?'

Faron notices that again he is directing the fragile, little body. It seems that it is only in moments of strong emotional situations that the spirit of Aideen takes over.

'You shouldn't smoke in here.'

'We'll just go into the garden then.' Faron goes and opens one of the French windows and heads out into the patio, Guida follows behind with the tray of refreshments.

She puts the try down on a small table, around which are several chairs, Faron goes to sit on one.

'You are not supposed to sit down.'

'Why not?'

'Because your calves are not yet accustomed to wearing heels and if you take the weight off of them for too long, when you stand up again the tendons will have tightened up again.'

'Look, I've been wearing these things for days now, and I'm only going to sit down long enough to have smoke and a drink.'

'It's your life.'

'Or was,' he smiles, sits and puts his feet up on another of the chairs.

'Guida?'

'Yes?'

'What am I supposed to say to the girls?'

'About what?'

'

About the fact that Luiz is Giuseppe's brother
and so is also a Duke, and that he might be the
oldest brother, so it should be he that marries
Casilda, and not Giuseppe.'

'What do you want to do?'

'I don't want to do anything, it just seems unfair
that Giuseppe and Tessa should suffer, if it is
really Luiz that is the oldest.'

'And what if he isn't?'

'Then everything will stay as it is.'

'So why don't you say something?'

'If I do, then Gianetta will hate me, but if I don't
and Tessa finds out that I knew, then she will
hate me.'

'Do you care?'

'Yes, yes I do.'

'Why should you care for these two women, you never cared for them in your life before?'

'Well I didn't know them before, I do know them now, and I don't want to hurt either of them.'

'Do you have to make a decision now?'

'No, it's just uncomfortable, that's all.'

'Why not give it until tomorrow, and then decide? A lot can happen before tomorrow.'

'Okay.'

'Don't stay out too long.'

'I won't, I'm finishing up this fag.' And the old woman takes the tray and wheezes her way off back into the house.

'The sun in the patio's summery warm, tomorrow belongs to me.' And with that, his arm drops to the side of the chair, the cigarette to the ground and his head to one side.

'Aideen!'

'Oh shit.' He gets up as quickly as he can. A burning, shooting pain erupts from his knees and down to his ankles.

'Shit, shit, shit, fuck, fuck, fuck.'

'Sit down!' Faron immediately does as he is told.

'Now stretch and flex your feet. Stretch, flex, stretch, flex, stretch, flex. Good. Now get up gently and keep your knees well bent, keep your weight mainly on your toes. Now, straighten your knees slightly, now bend again.

Now straighten more, and bend, and straighten and bend and straighten, more, now bend. Now straighten right up, bend, straighten, bend. Good.

Aideen, when I give you an instruction, I expect you to take notice and follow it to the letter.

Now you know why I said for you not to relax while wearing heels, it can take several weeks for your tendons to get used to stretching and relaxing so that you can take your heels off and on at will.'

'Sorry,' the naughty child has been caught doing a 'bêtise'.

'This time I feel that you have already suffered enough, and I hope that you have learned a valuable lesson in following instructions.'

'I will follow all your instructions in future,' she knew that that was the thing to say.

'Good, I see that you haven't fallen into the pool, yet. Please hurry and finish your chores, or else you will still not get any supper. You have just an hour before everyone else starts eating.'

'I'll be there.'

'I would expect so, for your sake.'

'Hi, ho, hi, ho it's off to work I go,' and taking the mop over his shoulder he heads back to the pool room. 'You've got the earrings, all that you lack, is a hook.

28. The Calm before the Storm

If one was to later ask, just when did it change, one would have to respond that it was during that afternoon of cleaning the ceiling of the pool room.

Whether it was finally feeling confident in the heels, the interaction with Marco or something different and intangible, it will never be possible to ascertain.

However, what is clear to see is that from that moment onwards there was a clear change in the attitude of Faron / Aideen. The straight back, forward glance and sure step, heralded a new beginning.

The change from prey to predator was clear for all to see …

'Aideen? What has happened?

'Hi, Tessa, how are you doing?'

'Oh, surviving, but you, you seem different, what's happened?'

'Don't know, don't care. What's to eat?'

'Oh there's a really nice vegi goulash.'

'Hi Gianetta, sure, I'll give it a try.'

'What's got into her?'

'I don't know, Tessa, but she seems a bit weird.'

'As if I don't have enough to worry about.'

'I know, honey, it's really so very unfair.'

'Let's not talk about it now, it's almost time to go and get dressed for tonight.'

'Oh don't you two leave me like that, I've just got my supper. Can't you stay with me for five minutes, pleeeasse?'

'We really should be getting ready.'

'Don't be so mean, Tessa, we can stay for another few minutes.'

'Okay, five minutes, by the watch.'

'Thanks, you're both sweet.'

'Gullible.'

'And gullible.'

'Aideen, how can you say that?'

'Easy Gi, even with a mouthful of meatless goulash.'

'Aideen?'

'Yes Gi?'

'Did Luiz say anything to you after we left? I know that there were just the two of you after Frenchy left.'

'No he didn't.'

'He didn't say anything to you.'

'No, he was a little distracted.'

'Distracted? Distracted by what?'

'By Giuseppe.'

'What was Giuseppe doing there?'

'Cool down Tess, he didn't hurt him.'

'Why would Giuseppe hurt Luiz?'

'Sweet child, why would Giuseppe possibly be upset about anything?'

'Was he drunk?'

'Do fish swim?'

'Yes.'

'Gi, it was a rhetorical question … that means a question that one does not expect an answer for … it's just like that.'

'Was he very drunk?'

'I think that he must have been drinking all night.'

'Oh my poor, poor love.'

'Did, did he attack Luiz?'

'I said that nothing bad happened. He just shouted at him.'

'What did he say?'

'Yes Aideen, please, please, what did he say?'

'Listen, it was none of my business so I walked away. And while we are on the subject of walking away, isn't it about time to go upstairs and get changed?'

'Tessa, she's right, we should go.'

'So let's go then.' And so they do.

29. Feelin' Groovy

Faron is feeling something that he hadn't felt for what seems the longest time.

Shower, shampoo, shave, starched shirt, slacks, suit jacket, splash of sultan of swing and swing into action.

Aideen's energy is exactly the female equivalent of that; shower, shampoo, shave, (legs in this case), short skirt, shiny top, splash of sin city, and ready to sashay into action.

He still needs to have Gianetta apply his makeup; that particular feminine art is still well beyond his fledgling competences. The Signora has insisted that he is made up by someone else, not to take the risk that he might appear, 'less than perfect'.

As soon as they are all ready, they elegantly descend the wide, gilded staircase.

Faron is intentionally, partially hidden by the other two, as he still has to correctly master the challenge of the steps, wearing the high heeled slippers, so carefully chosen for him.

They enter the ballroom, already starting to fill up with this evenings' clients and some of the other girls. Luiz and Giuseppe are on the mini stage, at the end, but have not yet begun to play.

Faron can well feel Aideen's excitement, they are scanning the room for something, or to be more exact, someone.

He is not to be found and the excitement gives place to increasing feelings of irritation and frustration.

The girls wonder off to look after their men, and Faron is left to 'look and to learn', hidden in a dark corner of the ornamental chamber.

'Nobody want to talk to you either?'

Faron turns round and almost falls off of his heels. Standing right next to him is … Casilda.

'No one wants to talk to me.'

'I suppose it's because of Tessa and Giuseppe.'

'As if it's my fault.'

What is with you women, because you are of the same sex, you treat me as your best friend and share your innermost secrets, without even a moment for introductions?

'Why are you telling me this?'

'Because you're new, because I've no-one to talk to, because, somewhere, I feel that I know and trust you, even though we've never spoken before.'

'Everyone says that it's your fault.'

'But I don't want to marry Giuseppe.'

'We know, you're in love with Marco.' Now it's Casilda's turn to look surprised.

'How do you know that?'

'I'm not supposed to leave this corner, please can you go and get me a drink, and then I'll tell you.'

Casilda is soon back with the aforementioned drink.

'Everyone had seen the way that you look at each other, and that, from time to time, you disappear off, somewhere.'

'It's that obvious?'

'You know, these girls are a little like horses in a box,' Casilda looks a little confused. 'They have very little to do all day, so they pass their time observing what the other horses are doing, or the behaviour of the humans.'

'And having nothing better to do than spy on us?'

'Exactly, having nothing better to do, watching you two lovebirds, became a general hobby.'

'I don't know whether I should slap you or pay you for such an information.'

'How about another drink?' The unexpected retort broke the heavy energy and Casilda broke into a relieved smile.

'Coming right up.'

'Thanks.'

'So why are you all giving me the cold shoulder?'

'I'm talking to you.'

'I spoke to you first.'

'I still replied.'

'Please, why?'

'It's called solidarity. Tessa has lost the love of her life, she will have her marriage dissolved, and he will marry you. How can we support her suffering and still be nice to you?'   Faron is having a little trouble following this train of thought, although he can see that there is some form of rational behind it.

'Oh.' It seems that Casilda has followed this logic without problem. 'And what about my suffering, and that of Marco?'

'Well, I suppose that we can be sorry for you, but Tessa is family.'

'And Marco and I are not?' Aideen hunches her shoulders in response.

'But what can I do?'

'You could elope with him, run away and get married.' No sooner has he said these words, than she realises what she has said. A feeling of idiotic panic fills their little body, he can almost hear her saying to herself; 'Oh my God, what have I done? If they do that, then I'll never get my chance with him.'

'We can't. Marco is an orphan, he was found by one of daddy's servants and brought to the house. The magistrate agreed to make him an indentured servant of our house until he celebrated his twenty first birthday.'

'And when will he be twenty one?' Tears start to well up in Casilda's eyes.

'Since no-one knew his age or birthday, daddy had the power to decide these things, he decided that he was to be four years old…'

'… but he is surely older than twenty one now.'

' … four years old on February the twenty ninth. And since he only celebrates his birthday once every four years, he will not be free until I'm eighty years old.'

'Oh.' Now it was Aideen that had information to digest.

'And an indentured servant, that runs away is a criminal that if caught can be imprisoned or even hanged.'

'So running away is not an option?'

'You see why I have to marry Giuseppe?'

'Yes, and Marco will have learn to live without you.'

'That's what makes me feel the most sad, I hate to think of him suffering.'

'Would, would, would it help if I was to keep him company a bit?'

'Would you? That would be so kind of you.'

'Well, now, you're almost like a friend, so I would be doing it for you. Do you know where he is?'

'No I don't. I'm afraid that he has gone off drinking, but if he comes here, I'll ask him to come and keep you company. Since you are forced to stay in this corner, it would be chivalrous of him to not let you have to stay all alone.'

'Then that would be a win, win situation for both of us.'

'I'll go and have a walk round and see if I can
see him.'

As she turns to leave, she faintly hears Aideen
singing quietly to herself, 'looking for fun, and
feeling groovy.'

30. The storm

There is something scarily wonderful about spiders. They work like crazy to spin there webs, but once the trap is set, they are the most patient of creatures. They just sit and wait, and wait, and wait. Knowing full well that sooner or later the unsuspecting fly will full into the shiny, sticky spun, and he will be hers.

Aideen is waiting patiently, the net is spun, helped by the poor, misled, innocent Casilda. Poor, innocent Casilda who will find Marco for her, and direct him directly into her parlour. Won't you step into my parlour, said the spider to the …

'Hello Aideen, Casilda said that I would find you here.'

'And so you've to rescue me from my solitary confinement?'

'I could keep you company for a while.'

'Then could you be an angel and go and get us both some drinks? It might be a good idea get a tray, then you wouldn't have to go back again.'

'I've already had quite a lot to drink tonight.'

'Listen, go and get the tray, anything that you spill because you're drunk, is just what you shouldn't drink.'

'That seems to make sense.'

'Of course it does, off you go.'

The bitch is getting him drunk. We certainly have things in common, we two.

Marco returns with the drinks.

'To loneliness.'

'Yes, to loneliness. Are you lonely too?'

'What do you think? The only people that I know here are Tessa, Gianetta and you.'

'And Casilda.'

'Yes, and Casilda, she's so very nice.'

'Yes, she's wonderful.'

'Yes, she is a very caring person. She is so concerned for you.'

'Is she?'

'Why, of course she is. Being betrothed to Giuseppe means that you will have no-one, and she is so worried that you will be sad.'

'How could I be otherwise?'

'Well, that is why she had the idea that you should come and look after me.'

'So that I wouldn't be unhappy?'

'Well, that was her idea. Of course, if I'm not helping you feel less unhappy, than maybe you shouldn't stay with me. It was just an idea after all.'

'I thought that I was to come to keep you company.'

'That was also true, but she was also thinking of your happiness. I am very happy that you are here to rescue me from my loneliness, just a woman without love.'

Marco is looking a little uncomfortable.

'But you don't have to stay if you don't want to, I really don't want to keep you.'

'And Casilda thought that being with you would be a good thing.'

'Maybe she was wrong, maybe you'd be happier talking to someone else.'

She notices that his glass is empty, so she passes him another drink, this is the fourth so far.

'I think that maybe I've had enough to drink.'

'You don't want me to be drinking alone now? That wouldn't be very gentlemanly of you.' He takes the drink.

'It is a warm in here, do you think that it would be okay if you escorted me out into the garden for a few moments?'

He stops to think for a moment before answering.

'Well, I don't see what harm that could be.'

'Let's go then.' They slip, unobserved out, into the walled garden.

'You'll have to help me walk over these tiles, you know that I've never worn heels before this week.'

'No?'

'No, I'm just a simple girl from the country.' He takes her arm and leads her out of the building. Almost immediately she stumbles and catches herself around his neck.

'Ow, oh, I'm so sorry. Such luck that you are so strong. Faron can feel his pulse quickening and his breath becoming shorter and quicker. 'So not used to these shoes, could you carry me to that bench?'

He carries her over to the first bench and slowly lowers her down onto it.

'Come sit with me please.'

'Casilda…'

'Is betrothed to Giuseppe, and you cannot do anything about it. You cannot even elope together.'

'She told you that?'

'She asked me to look after you. To help you to forget her.'

'I cannot forget her.'

'You must. You know full well that what is hurting her most at this time is the idea that you are suffering.'

'She is so sweet and caring.'

'Exactly, that is why she has asked me if I would remind you that there are other girls that you could love.'

'I'm not following you.'

'She asked me to get you to make love to me.' Her breathing was so shallow that Faron was scared that they would faint, but fainting didn't seem to be that likely.

'You are not joking are you?'

'Listen, you know her better than I do, is that something that she might think of to get you to suffer less?'

'But that would be a betrayal.'

'Not if it was her wish. Do you want to go and ask her, here now in the ballroom? It might be a bit uncomfortable for her to say to you, but please go ahead and ask if you need to.'

'No, I couldn't do that.'

'She did send you to me, didn't she?'

'Yes she did.'

'So why do you think she would do that, if not for me to distract you?'

'To keep you company.'

'Did I really look like I needed company? Or did I look happy and relaxed? *Spider!*

'Yes, she sent me to you.'

'Then let's do what she asked.' Faron watches as she tilts his head closer and closer to Marco's. Their eyes meet, she half smiles, arches her back to raise her mouth closer and closer to his.

She has almost stopped breathing altogether, her whole body tense, closer, closer. He doesn't move, not one inch, not even a centimetre, but allows for the advance.

The pair of lips touch and compress, like two slow motion railway carriages, joining together, the buffers absorbing all impact, as they come gently together for coupling.

Faron is taken by the vibrant buzzing over his whole body. There is no need to breath, no need to see, no need to hear, just being here, with him, at last, is all that life needs to be.

He becomes taken by the kiss, and as if controlled by some low level human programming, his arms slide round and envelope her body. 'Hold me, hold me tight, tighter,' he can hear her screaming from inside.

To be kissing a man, to be hugged by a man, to be safe and protected and lost in a man's arms; these are firsts for Faron, but more is to follow.

Her breasts are beginning to slightly swell, he can feel them becoming taunt, and the nipples to harden and protrude, like two miniature penis's becoming erect and sensitive.

And just like his erect member, there is a deep and immediate need to have them touched and caressed.

She slides her hands behind her back and drags Marco's hands onto her gently throbbing breasts. The touch, totally stops her breath, the most exquisite, pleasure and pain, the sensation is so very intense.

It is this point that he becomes acutely aware of the heat and wetness in his vagina.

Heat, wetness, swelling and throbbing, as if the under part of his shaft and penis head have become flattened and spread all around, inside and outside of his sexual region.

To have it stroked, caressed, teased, and good God yes, penetrated was becoming the only aim in life.

She grabs his hand again and this time, shamelessly plunges it between her legs.

The gesture alone, with the single passing stroke, creates a wave of intense pleasure, he can feel her toes curling up with the excitement. Heaven only knows what he is going to experience when she is entered and arrives at orgasm.

At the same she tests out the size of his manhood with her own hands. Just the idea of taking it out, stroking it and fondling it shoots another electric wave through her over excited body.

Marco, himself is now being carried on the crest of the female sexual wave of excitement and desire.

Both are now committed to the race, the race to copulation and climax.

'Aideen, I don't think that that is the type of observation that the Signora was planning for you for tonight.'

The two guilty children break away from each, pulling back their hands, as if by quickly extracting them from the cookie jar will make it seem that they were never in it.

 'Marco, I do believe that Colonel Pavoneggiarsi is looking for you inside.' He goes to help Aideen to her feet.

'Aideen would do better to not enter with you, she will wait for a moment and come back inside with me.'

He looks slightly angrily at the old woman, shrugs his shoulders and re-enters the building.

'Why did you do that? I'm here to learn about pleasure, and that was exactly what I was doing!' Faron is more than a little upset.

'You are not here for that.'

'Fuck you, I'm going to bed to play with myself, and that you can't stop me doing.'

And with her head high, she leaves the old guide sadly shaking her grisly, grey head as the even older grey moon reflects coldly on all this.

31. Part of their World

Faron wakes up to find a skimpy bathing suit hanging on the chair next to his bed.

'What's that for?'

'You could wipe your nose with it.'

'Tessa.'

'I know, don't be mean.'

'Are we going swimming?' Faron could feel a simple, pure, innocent excitement filling his little body.

'It's a swimming morning, we get to use the pool and take breakfast on the terrace.'

'One of the perks of the job,' adds Tessa.

'And no heels,' Faron laughs as they quickly dress and rush down stairs like a group of giggly school girls.

The sun is already up and warming the tiles. The girls are sipping fruit cocktails and nibbling bits of raw fruit, the atmosphere is one of summer holidays.

The Venice beaches must already be filling with school kids on holiday and tourists taking a break from the regular site seeing tours.

Tessa is clearly doing her best to join in to not spoil the morning for the others, this is strangely obvious for Faron. As with most men, the inner lives of the fairer sex have always been a sometimes wonderful, sometimes scary secret from him. However, now linked to the feminine sensitivity of Aideen, this is as clear as if she had written it in large letters and stapled it to her forehead.

What is equally clear, but much less easy to understand are the feelings of real happiness and joy that he is capturing coming from Gianetta. Even such a perception would normally evoke little more than a faint stirring of curiosity, but not that of his inquisitive host.

It still takes a good half hour before Gianetta can be cornered close to the far wall of the terrace, far, far away from other inquisitive eyes and ears.

'What's up?'

'Nothing,' she answers, defensively.

'Gi, look, I might be the new girl here, but I've lived a while on the streets, and I can smell when something's up. So you might as well admit it, it looks like you've swallowed the Cheshire Cat.'

'Oh no, do you think that anyone else has noticed? Did Tessa say anything to you?'

'So far it seems that everyone is too busy having fun to bother about you, and Tessa is working hard to fit in, so she's acting like she's totally high on something. No, for the moment, I don't think that anyone else has noticed.'

'Oh thank God, she mustn't find out. At least not for now.'

'So?'

'You promise not to tell her.'

'Who, the Signora?'

'No, not her, she's not important. Tessa.'

'I mustn't tell Tessa?'

'Please, please, you must promise, promise, promise me that if I tell you then you will keep it a secret.'

'Sure, I'm good.'

'Last night, after the others had gone, Luiz and I came out here and had a talk. I asked him if he had thought about what he would do when Giuseppe marries Casilda. If he would carry on playing, or what. So he then looked at me in a strange way.

'I wouldn't worry too much about that if I were you.' He replies with a weird look.

'Why are you looking at me that way?' I asked him. I was a bit troubled.

'Because our future is taken care of,' he says

'What are you talking about?' I started to panic, I had all scary ideas in my head like he was going to rob a bank or something.

'We're going to be rich,' he continues.

'What are you planning to do?' I was getting really scared.

'Do? I'm not going to do anything. Other than claim my heritage.' He smiles again, I'm really lost here.

'What heritage?' So lost. He doesn't answer for a moment, but gently takes my hand, lifts it to his mouth and kisses my wedding ring.

'This ring, with which we have been wed, is the twin of Giuseppe's.' I'm not understanding anything. I'm not always very quick to understand everything, you know.

'Giuseppe is a Duke,' he says, 'I have the same ring, so I am the Duke's brother.

As soon as he and Casilda are married, I will present us as members of the royal family, we can be like them, part of that world. We will have a share in all the properties and fortune of the Dukedom.'

'Why don't you tell them now?' I asked.

'Because no one really knows if we're twins or if not who's the oldest. So if I tell them now, maybe they well think that I'm the oldest, and then it will be me that has to marry Casilda.'

'No, they wouldn't.' I was really, really scared.

'Which is why we must keep it a secret until after the marriage, then it will be too late. No-body must know.' He then looked at me in a really serious way. 'You understand, no-body.'

And so, I mustn't tell anyone, but I've told you.'

'It's okay, Gi, I'll keep your secret, even from Tessa.'

'You, you're a really, really good friend.'

'I'm an idiot to have myself mixed up in this.' *So now you realise that.* 'Come, let's get back to pool before anyone realises that we've been gone so long and starts to ask questions.'

'Race you back.'

'Last one in the pool's a duck.'   And off they run.

32. Heaven can wait

Lunch is over, Faron is wearing a short print dress and his usual high heeled pumps.

'Today you will have the pleasant task of polishing the banisters of the staircase.'

'Don't you pay a cleaning woman for that?' Faron was starting to become irritated by the continuing mundane tasks that he was being asked to perform.

'Aideen, I'm sorry that you would think to question my methods. Please return to your room, pack your meagre belongings, then remove yourself from this establishment post haste.'

'What? What? You can't just throw me out, not just like that.'

'Can't I?'

'But, but, but I don't want to go. Please don't make me go. Please, please, Signora, I've no place to go, and I've got friends here. Please.' Aideen was sobbing, almost uncontrollably.

'Aideen, do you want to stay?'

'Yes, yes, yes please.'

'Then go and dry your eyes, get yourself a drink of water and be back here in five minutes so I can explain exactly how I want you to do this job.'

She is back in less than the five minutes allotted.

'You will do exactly as I say. Take the cloth in your left hand, the wax bucket in the other. You will start here at the bottom step. Dip the cloth in the wax, straighten up, back straight, head up facing forward, rub the wax onto the wood.

No! do not look at the banister, keep looking forward. Yes, good, that is better, right. Now take a step, keeping your weight on your toes, good. Now wax, keeping your head looking forward, neither to the left, and never ever down.

When you have waxed on the left banister, you will continue across and do the same with the right, while descending the steps. Please go up some steps and cross over to the right.

Now please show me how you will wax this one. Good, now down a step, stop, stop, stop. Your back must remain absolutely straight; head looking forward, legs stay close together, bend from the knee, weight on the heel.

That's it. Don't worry if you need to use the banister for support to begin with. Again, head high, think that are a princess, back straight, remember cleaning the pillars, let your body drop vertically, onto the heel, and there you are. I'll be back to check up on you later.'

Princess? More like fucking Cinderella.

And so Faron gets to work applying the soft, sweet smelling wax to the smooth, wooden banister rails.

Heels, click, click, clicking on the golden threaded, marble steps.

He is becoming unhappily, accustomed to these mindless tasks, but she has made it painfully clear, 'do as I say, without question or hesitation, or else…, out.'

I suppose that somewhere it's a matter of life and death.

And he finds a way to amuse himself imagining that he is climbing the stairs up, all the way to heaven. So as to defend himself from a court of American immigrants that want him to be dead, but he will find clever, twisted arguments so as prove that he must be allowed to return back to earth. Smiling at the possible parallel with his own real situation.

And then, suddenly, he is started to descend, to return to the earth, down the stairs, head high, back straight, proud and tall. He has won.

'Congratulations, very well done.' Shocked that he hasn't noticed her entrance, but on reflection, not so very much.

'Am I done then?'

'For waxing, yes, that seems quite adequate. Since you have done so well, you may take a break before you polish it off.'

'Polish it off?'

'Well we can't leave it on, can we now?'

'No, no, I suppose not.'

'Guida is coming with some lemonade, you can have a ten minutes break. If you must smoke, please do not leave the tips by the door.' And she turns and leaves.

'I think that she is quite pleased with your progress.'

'What, as a house maid?'

'Must be, you don't seem to be doing anything else useful.'

'I feel like taking this lemonade and pouring over your ugly, little, grey head.'

'Did you want a cigarette then?'

'No, I'll just drink this and get back to it. The quicker that I start, the quicker it'll be finished.'

He then finishes his drink, picks up a second cloth, turns back to the stairs and starts to polish off the wax.

33.Soapsuds and Secrets

Faron asks to be excused for the evening feigning a headache. As the girls are usually excused if they are coming on their periods, this request was understood as such and the accord is discretely given.

Faron is open to pass the time taking a very long bath, luxuriating in the hot scented water, a deep cleansing face mask, hair shampooed and in the process of a long conditioning. Nothing to worry about, no one to pressure him to do this or that, an evening of peace and relaxation.

Until.

The door opens and immediately slams shut, moments later, it opens again, someone enters, the door is closed softly.

After having lived in close proximity with the other girls for a few days now, Faron has lost the habit to close and lock the door. Actually, the girls rarely close the door unless they are going to the toilet, and then not even always.

So, in this particular instance, it is not surprising that the bathroom door is ajar and when the girls start talking, he can clearly hear all that is being said.

'I can't stand it anymore.'

'It'll be alright.'

'No it won't, and well you know it. He'll marry that bitch, and they'll both live, 'happy ever after' in there big castle, wanting for nothing. And me, what about me? I'll be stuck here, stuck in this fucking whore house for the rest of my life. Is that it? Is that all that I can look forward to, becoming a prostitute like all the others? Giving my body for a few euros, just long enough to get old and haggard. And finally, finally to get myself a miserable flat and try and grab one or two old clients to help me pay the rent and feed myself until I die an old and lonely hag?'

'It won't be like that.'

'Why won't it be like that? How many of the girls that we've known have succeeded to get out of this rat hole?'

'….'

'So, do you have a magic trick? Or are counting on your wonderful Luiz to be discovered as the next Vivaldi and become super known and super rich and take you away from all this?'

'Don't talk like that. Please don't talk like that.'

'You know that are poisons that act real quick and don't hurt at all.'

'Tessa, what are you talking about?'

'I'm talking about a way out. I'm not going to stay here and be used by those filthy drunks, like some faceless sex toy. At least I can go out with a bit of dignity.'

'Tessa, you must never think of doing such a thing.'

'Why not, I've not got a million other options.'

'You can come with us.'

'What? Come with you two? You've hardly enough to get off of island.'

'Not yet, but that will change.'

'Sure, just as soon as when Hell freezes over.'

'No, not at all.'

'Listen, Luiz is sweet, he's cute, he's even a fairly good musician, but he'll never be rich, so maybe you should just stop dreaming of it. You'll only end up disappointed.'

'We're going to be rich.'

'Yeh sure, and I'm a princess in disguise.'

'Luiz is a Duke.'

'No honey, it's Giuseppe that's the Duke, Luiz is just, just, just Luiz.'

'Show me your hand. No, the one with the ring. Now look at this.'

'Why, you're ring, it's the same as mine, I've never noticed that before.'

' 'Cus you've never bothered to look. Yes, Luiz had the same ring on a cord round his neck, the same as Giuseppe. He's Giuseppe's brother. As soon as Giuseppe is married, then Luiz will declare himself as his brother, and we'll be rich.'

'Luiz is Giuseppe's brother?'

'And when we get rich, you can come with us. Tessa, we'll take care of you. I've already talked it over with Luiz and he totally agrees.'

'But if he is Giuseppe's brother then maybe he's the oldest.'

'Please Tessa, I promised not to tell anyone until after the marriage, please, please don't tell anyone. I know that you would want to try and get Casilda to marry Luiz, but I couldn't take the risk that you would kill yourself before I could tell you.'

'So you risked telling me, even if it might have meant that you would have lost Luiz?'

'You are the closest thing that I have got to a sister, I couldn't take the risk.'

'Where's Aideen?'

'Aideen?'

'Here, in the bath.'

Tessa rushes in to bathroom.

'Aideen, did you hear what we were talking about?'

'No sweat, sister, nothing that I didn't already know.'

'Gi?'

'I had to tell her this afternoon, she knew that there was something up. I think that she must have been a witch in a past life.'

'Is it a secret then?'

'I'm good.'

'Thanks Aideen, Tessa?'

'How could I rat out on my sister?'

'I've a bottle of white somewhere, who's for a drink?'

34. Showing the Cat her Claws

'So what do you think that I'll get to clean today?'

They are at breakfast, Faron has finished several slices of a particularly sweet honey melon and is waiting for the magical appearance of the beautiful step-mother to come and instruct him as to this morning's tasks.

'Tessa, you will accompany Aideen to Madame Mimm's, you could with a bit of tidying up. Well get a move on, she hasn't get all day, she has other clients to take care of. The appointment is in my name as usual, you might think to leave a little tip, it would be elegant.'

'Where are we going''

'Madame Mimm's magic shop.'

'Magic?'

'Don't panic, it's just a figure of speech, but she does do a type of magic.'

'What type?'

'Nothing to worry about. Wow, you're doing really well?'

'What?'

'I don't know how you've done it, but I could never have learnt to walk in heels as quickly as you have, bloody miracle.'

Faron stops for the shortest of seconds, he had totally forgotten that he was wearing his high heel pumps, even the frequent humped backed Venetian bridges had not awakened his attention.

'You're right, I seem to have got it.'

'Good on ya' girl. Here we go.' They arrive before a gaudily decorated shop front, which reads in huge, multi-coloured letters – 'Madame Mimm's Magic Shop, Beauty Salon.' And in slightly smaller letters underneath, 'Difficult cases treated immediately, please allow more time for miracles.'

'What are we going to do in here?'

'Well you are not here to sweep up. Just come in and relax and enjoy. I don't suppose that you've the habit of having your nails done.'

'I had a manicure once.'

'Well, it's like that, and a bit more.' Faron and Tessa find themselves places to wait and flip through the pile of magazines while waiting. The ambiance is warm and friendly, they are offered a coffee and, although it seems acceptable to smoke in the magic shop, they take their coffee and cigarette out for a smoke.

'Are you okay with the whole Giuseppe and Casilda, and Luiz and Gianetta thing?' *Why in Heaven's name would you want to open that can o' worms again. Stupid bitch!*

'Of course not, but Gi's a good girl, not the brightest of our sex, but she's good and honest. I wish that there was some other way out, but I can't think of anything for the moment.'

'It just doesn't seem fair.'

'Thanks, but I have decided that that is the way that it should be.'

'But if Luiz is older than Giuseppe.'

'Nobody knows, he might be, or he might not, they might even be non-identical twins, really, no one knows.'   They finish their coffee and cigarettes and return to the interior.

'What are those?' The assistant has just brought a pad, on which are ten long, red claws.

'Is there something wrong, dear?' Madame Mimm is a ball of friendly, energy, and the term as totally accurate. She is particularly short, Munchkin height, but of exactly the same diameter in all directions.

'The, there, those, those, things, they're not for me are they?'

'Why of course they are my dear, exactly as ordered.'

'But you are going to file them down a bit, aren't you?' Faron is truly concerned, the nails are objectively huge.

'A little bit, don't you worry, everything will be fine.'

But things were not fine, Faron exists the shop sporting an enormous paw of extended claws.

'What am I supposed to do with these?' He waves his hand helplessly.

'Careful!'

'Sorry Tessa, but look at these bloody things, I'm not going to be able to do anything with things stuck on my hands.'

'The Signora must have a good reason for this.'

'It's revenge, she knows that I have to do everything that she says or I'm to be thrown out on the street.'

'Why should she want revenge on you? Don't forget, she's still got that bet with the Colonel.'

'Exactly, she's done nothing to get me ready for tomorrow night and she knows that she's going to lose the bet, so she's taking it out on me.'

'I'm really not sure about that. If she didn't think that she, you could pull it off, she wouldn't have taken the bet. And, more than that, if she already knew that you couldn't do it, she wouldn't still be wasting her time and money on you, you'd already be out.'

'I suppose that maybe you're right, but that still doesn't explain these.'

'Could you just wave them about here, they make a great pair of fans.'

'I'm going to get you for that.' And the two girls run off, squealing with laughter.

35.All that glitters

Eating lunch was no picnic! Faron feels that he is a character in a Bosch painting, in some Hellish feast, where there is a wonderful feast spread out, here, in front of him, but he is incapable to eat the food.

Eventually he manages to find a way to handle the knife and fork. The trick is to somehow flatten his fingers so that the nails pass over the sides of the cutlery. He appreciates the attention of the other girls that help him to acquire this non-obvious manoeuvre.

'Aideen, please come here. Let me see, yes, that is as I had instructed.'

'Why?'

'Pardon?'

'Why have you asked her to put on such big nails? None of the others have such long nails.'

'Yours is to do or die, not ask why. … Understood?'

'Yes ma'am.'

'Good, I'm glad that we understand each other. You are to report back here in twenty minutes and I will show you your task for the afternoon.'

I won't be able to do much with things on my hands.

'Did you say something, Aideen?'

'I said that I will be back soon.'

'Do.'

… The girls arrive at their room.

'Do either of you two understand her?'

'I don't always understand things, Tessa?'

'Sorry Aideen, God works in mysterious ways. Isn't it time to return back down stairs?'

'Yeh, I suppose so, catch you both later.'

She descends the gold veined staircase, intrigued but not particularly eager to see what would be in store for her, for this afternoon.

The dining table is piled with silverware. There is a large bottle containing some brown sort of liquid and two piles of cloths.

'Hello Aideen, right on time, good girl.'

'What am I supposed to do with those?'

'I understand that it is termed as polishing.' She smiles at Aideen in a strangely friendly fashion.

'With the cloths on this side, you pour some of this cleaning fluid onto a cloth, then you rub it all over the object. Then with a clean cloth, from this pile, you then rub it off, and that, so it seems, is how you polish silver.'

'But how am I supposed to do that, wearing these?'

'The same as you managed to eat your dinner. You are a very resourceful young lady, you will manage, I'm sure of it. I'll be back later to look in on you. Enjoy.'

'This is rubbish, it's impossible.'

'Nothing is impossible.'

'It's easy for you say, you're not Hercules.'

'And you are?'

'Well it seems a little like that.'

'Come, we know that you can do this.'

'Can't you help me?'

'It's more than my job's worth?'

'What do you mean, more than your job's worth? This isn't your job, you're a guide, this world isn't even real. Can't you just take us somewhere else?'

'Soon Faron, you've nearly learned that which you must learn here.'

'But what about the polishing?'

'Polish on, polish off.'

'Big help, you are.'

'I do my best.' And Faron sets himself towards the job in hand. It takes quite a lot of time, effort and swearing before he finds the techniques and acquires the habit to pick up the bottle, pour the liquid onto the cloth, pick up the cutlery, rub the cloth onto the object, change cloths, rub the cleaner off and put down the object.

After all, it doesn't turn out to be such a difficult or unpleasant task.

'Finished already?'

'Do you have any more that needs doing?'

'No, that's fine for now, thank you Aideen. We will be entertaining tonight and I will require your participation, so go and take some time for yourself. And I would also suggest that you go to the kitchen and find yourself a snack.'

No less confused than usual, Faron goes to the kitchen where he sneaks himself his first sandwich in a week.

'What's happening tonight, Tess?' He is again in the bedroom with the others.

'We're invited to dine with the Signora and her guests.'

'Then why was I told to go and get something from the kitchen?'

'Beats me, maybe you'll be serving us dinner.'

'Tessa!'

' … don't be mean.'

But she wasn't wrong.

36. Your servants serve you right

Tessa was in fact totally right, Aideen was taken into the kitchen, given an apron and, very quickly, instructed on what is expected of a serving girl.

The tray was to be carried on her right hand, the serving utensils in the left hand. Service moves in a single direction. Food service proceeds to the right, counter clockwise, starting with the guest of honour. Beverage service progresses to the left, clockwise.

Plates are served and cleared from the left side. The server's right hand clears a used plate, and the left hand slides a fresh plate into place. Beverages are served and cleared from the right side.

The guests are already seated at the table when he brings in the salad platter.

Faron is a little surprised to see who Signora Mallevaichi has chosen to invite for this particular evening. The guest of honour is, not surprisingly, the Colonel, he is accompanied by his daughter, Casilda. Then there is her husband-to-be, Giuseppe, but also Tessa and Gianetta.

Twisted bitch, you just love to play with people, don't you?

'Aideen, you must keep you back straight, your posture is very, very important. There, that's better, much better. It is most kind of you Aideen to fill in for tonight, it is most unfortunate that Mary is unwell this evening.'

Faron passes first to the Colonel, it is weird for him to see his father once more at the dinner table, and he is shocked, but not really surprised to notice a cut glass, crystal whiskey glass, resting by his right hand.

'Salad, colonel?'

'Oh, no thank you m' dear, not tonight.' Faron is having some difficulty balancing the tray and serving the food, especially since he is still slightly ill at ease with his finger enhancements.

The meal passes in a civilised manner and Faron succeeds to serve the meal without mishap, and looks to be going well. Until he returns with the dessert tray …

'So who shall we ask to be the bride of honour for the wedding? What do you think Colonel, that we ask Tessa here, I'm sure that she would be most suitable?'

'Thank you ma'am, but I'd rather not.'

'But I thought that you were such a good friend of both Casilda and Giuseppe.'

'I just would rather not.' Tessa's eyes begin to well up.

'Is there something wrong, m' dear?' He seems to be honestly ignorant of the true situation.

'She's just a bit tired ma'am, can we please be excused?'

'Yet quite yet, Gianetta, Aideen has just brought in the desserts, it would be impolite to leave just now.'

'So you don't want to be my maid of honour, for my marriage to Giuseppe?'

Something snapped in Aideen, it was bad enough for Maman to goad Tessa, but have Casilda jump in and add insult to injury, well that was just much.

Faron feared that something bad was going to happen, but when Aideen decided to say or do something, he had no choice but to just wait, watch and hope that it would be okay.

'Casilda cannot marry Giuseppe.' *Oh shit!*

'What was that Aideen.' She had got everyone's attention.

'I think that everyone heard me, correctly, ma'am, Casilda cannot marry Giuseppe.'

'And exactly why cannot my daughter my Giuseppe?'

'Because Giuseppe is not the only son of the Duke.'

'Aideen!' Tessa, Gianetta and Giuseppe, all shouted in unison.

'Aideen, please put that try down before you pour chocolate sauce down someone's neck. Thank you. Now if you please, I wish for you to explain yourself.

'Please, please Aideen no,' now it was Gianetta who was in tears.

'Continue Aideen.'

'Yes ma'am. Luiz is also a son of the Duke.'

'Do you have proof of this assertion?'

'Yes sir, if you would just care to look at her hand, her wedding ring is identical to that of Tessa's.' The colonel makes a gesture to Gianetta, who reluctantly shows him her ring.

'Well, then, it will just have to be like that. Casilda, we have a slight change of plans, you will not marry Giuseppe, but Luiz.'

'Casilda cannot marry Luiz, either.'

'What is it now, Aideen?'

'I'm sorry Casilda, but you just can't marry Luiz either.'

'Why not? I'm to marry one or the other.'

'Aideen, please would you like to share your thoughts with us?' Maman was using her sweetest voice,

Faron knew this tone well, it always masked something, exactly what, he rarely found out, but there was always something lurking in the back of her twisted mind.

'As they were both thought to be orphans, no one knows who is the elder, or even if they are both twins. So it is impossible to know which of the two was betrothed to Casilda. There is no law that can force someone to marry if there is no way to prove if it is in fact that person that was betrothed in the first place.'

It took a moment or two for the facts to sink in.

'Neither Luiz nor I can be forced to marry Casilda?'

'I don't think so.'

'Aideen, I love you.' Tessa jumps to her feet and hurls herself towards Aideen. Gianetta, being slightly slower on the uptake takes a few moments to react.

'I'm still married to Luiz, then?'

'For the moment.' Time stops and everyone turns round to stare at Maman.

'Please will everyone sit down, Aideen, please bring yourself a chair, I have something to share.'

Faron goes to get a chair and joins the others at the table.

'A good few years ago, I received a message from the Duke of Burgundy, it seems that there was an uprising in his domain and that he was scared for his family. That he was sending a nurse here to Venice because he felt this was one of the most secure places to leave his progeny, and that I was to help her in any way that she might ask.

Some days later there was woman at my door asking for a sum of money as the Duke had not succeeded to organise food and lodging for her. I gave her what she asked for, and sent her on her way. I was too discreet to ask about what happened to the child or children, imagining that they would be safest, the fewest people knew of the secret.'

'You mean that you have always known the whereabouts of the Dukes children?'

'No colonel, I never chose to ask.'

'But you know that I have been looking for him for years.'

'The Duke wrote to me in confidence, I'm sure that you must understand, being as you are, a man of honour, that I could never break a confidence of that sort.'

'I apologise, you are quite right, you were honour bound to keep their secret and her identity also.'

'But now that we know who they are, I feel that I no longer have to keep her hidden. I feel it only correct that we find out which of the two are the eldest, so that your daughter can marry and the betrothal respected.'

'Then call for her and tomorrow we can make the official announcement of the wedding.'

'I will see to it. Please send for Marco, I will send him with the message.'

And so she does.

The girls leave the table in silence, go up the stairs in silence, undress in silence, wash off their makeup in silence, and go to bed, in silence.

37. When shall we three meet again?

The morning was bright and cheerful, as were the birds and more than likely also the bees. Unfortunately the same can not be said for the residents of the small room, named as virgin territory.

The ice cold silence that had reigned the previous evening had in no way thawed through the night.

They get up in silence, wash in silence, dress in silence, put on their makeup in silence, (Gianetta is still obliged to see to Aideen), and descend in exquisite silence.

As soon as they arrive at the breakfast table, the two others waste no time to find other girls to eat with.

Saturday morning is a free morning for Faron, he has no obligations, but neither does he have any plans. Not feeling particularly ready to eat, he borrows a cigarette and goes outside the front door to have a smoke and try and work out what to do next.

'Fancy and coffee and doughnut?'

'You know that I don't have any cash.'

'This time I can treat you.'

They are now gently strolling down the Riva degli Schiavoni, they are going to have a breakfast in one of the pasticcerias in the Piazza San Marco.

Faron is struck by the strong feeling of déjà vu due to the exact repetition of the same situation, a situation that seems months away in the past, but yet is really less than a week.

As if in the weirdest of dreams, even more weird than the dream that he is already experiencing, they enter the same coffee shop that he entered before he had become aware that he had been transformed into Aideen.

'Let's sit over here', sitting in the same corner, seems to be poetic. The guide has to turn sideways to pass his fat, little body between the tightly packed tables.

'I don't suppose if I was to look at myself again in the window, that I would be magically changed back into myself?'

'Why would you want to do that, tonight is your big night?'

'Big night, big disaster, that's what it's going to be. Maman has taught me nothing, I'm totally unprepared to be shown off in public, so I'll just make a total fool of myself.

And worse than that, I've screwed up totally my relationship with the girls and their own chances of happiness. What's the point of hanging around, I'm just as much a screw-up as I was when I topped myself in the real world.'

'Do you really believe that?'

'I wouldn't be saying it otherwise.'

'Faron, trust me, if you run out now, again, you'll never know what might happen.'

'But I don't want to know what will happen. Don't you understand, I don't want to find out what is going to happen, because it's going to be shit.'

'Please hear me out, okay?'

'Sure, just keep the coffee coming.'

'You are here to learn a lesson.'

'Sure, I'm the world's greatest fuck-up.'

'This island, this world and all that is in it has been created so that you might have certain experiences. If it all fails, it doesn't really matter, as it will all fade when you leave.'

'So what's the point?'

'The point will be clear for you by tomorrow morning.'

'And then I can bugger off.'

'Yes, then you can bugger off, as you so colourfully express it.'

'No matter what happens?'

'Just as long as you do your best to do as you are asked.'

'And if I don't?'

'Then I cannot promise that you have learned the lesson.'

'And I will have to stay until I do?'

'I suppose so.'

'You don't know?'

'I'm not God.'

'Oh yes, I remember,' and thinking back to that first evening suddenly made him smile, 'okay, I'll play along with this charade for just a little bit longer.'

'Good.'

'But will I be able to make the girls like me again?'

'Is it important for you?'

'Yes, I suppose that it is.'

'Then let's hope that you can.'

They leave the coffee shop and stroll around canals until lunch time.

38.A time of red and black

Faron eats alone, one or two of the girls make as if to come close and join him, but before they can advance more than a few steps, another girl passes or crosses or coughs or whatever signal that needs to pass to confirm that that would not be a good idea.

In a way Faron is more comfortable not having to interact with any them, but of course that is not to last.

'Tessa, your points are a mess, you will go and get them seen to. Oh, and you can take Aideen with you, something needs to done with her hair before tonight. …. Is there a problem, Tessa?'

'No, no problem.'

'Good, you will both leave immediately, you are expected.'

No words are passed until they are well on their way.

'I hate her.'

'More than me?'

'You are not worth hating, you're too stupid.'

'I was only trying to help.'

'You don't understand, she's just playing with us, all of us.'

'I don't understand.'

'Of course you don't, how could you, you're just a child off of the street.'

'Please, please tell me, I'd like to understand.'

'She's like that cat, you know Lucifer, she's like Lucifer.'

'Who's Lucifer?'

'I told you, a cat, a bad cat, hateful. She's just like him, just likes to play cat and mouse with people. … At the table last night, she chose use to see what she could get us to do, and you, you idiot, you fell totally into her trap.'

'But she couldn't know about the ring.'

'Why wouldn't she, she notices everything. You don't think that she's not capable to notice that Gi and I have identical rings?'

'But she couldn't know that I would say anything.'

'No, but she planned that if she goaded us enough, one of us would crack and that we'd reveal the truth.'

'But if she already knew, why not just tell everyone?'

'What would be the fun in that? The game was to get one of us to betray the other.'

'But I didn't mean to betray anyone, I was only trying to help.'

Again Faron has no control on the wave of emotion that submerges his fragile body. The tears well up and flow out on the tidal wave of sadness and despair.

'I wanted to help, and now I've spoilt it for everyone, and now you all hate me.'

'Aideen, it's alright.'

'No it's not, nobody will talk to me.'

'It'll pass, it's just that we are all scared for Gi.'

'What do you mean?'

'I'm a survivor, but Gi is more fragile. If Luiz has to marry Casilda, it would be very hard on her.'

'Poor Gi.'

'We'll just have to wait until tonight and see what happens. Here we are.'

They enter a small hair salon. A tall brunette welcomes them.

'Hi Tessa, what's up? I suppose that you're Aideen, come on in. We'll get you washed in a mo', fancy a coffee?'

'That would be great.'

'You too, Aideen?'

'Yes please.'

'Fine, just wait over there.' The coffees arrived and were drunk, neither girl felt like continuing the conversation where they might be overheard, so they just leafed through the magazines and waited their turns to have their hair washed.

'So Aideen, you want to add some colour to your hair?'

'Do I?'

'Well, that's what I was asked to do. This is your hair isn't it?' She shows Faron some strands of bright red hair, exactly the same as his own.

'It looks like mine.'

'Of course it is. I've already done the colour test, and it's all good. Now you just relax and I'll see to making you even more beautiful than you already are.'

She stuffs Faron's mess of hair into a clear plastic skull cap. Totally fascinated, Faron doesn't say a word. She then proceeds to poke and extract random strands of out from the cap.

'Time for the witches brew,' and off she goes to get a steaming beaker of thick, black goo, which she thickly applies with a large brush.

'There we go, now just to wrap you up,' she then proceeds to wrap his head in several layers of transparent food wrap. 'Fancy another coffee?'

'Sure,' the coffee arrives about the same time as a dangerous looking object with various rings, on a movable stand. In fact, it is no more sinister than a form of hair dryer.

Time passes, Faron fades in and out of dreams, until the film and the cap are gently removed. His hair is slightly trimmed, brushed and sprayed.

'Wow, not bad.'

'What do you think?' Faron is also impressed.

'It's wonderful, who'd have thought that adding some black lowlights would look so good?'

'Who indeed?'

'Oh yes, Lucifer.' And for some reason, unknown even to themselves, they suddenly both burst out laughing.

'Best of luck for tonight.'

'Thanks so much, it's wonderful.'

'Yes I know, I'm really good. Bye.' And off they go, Aideen's 'coming out', is waiting for her.

39. Find the Duke

Faron returns to find several surprises waiting for him. The first is … Madame Mimm.

'Sit', and without a word, she takes Faron's nails and trims them to about a half of the original length. 'Perfect, have a wonderful evening Aideen.'

Next, he finds a pretty, red and black, off the shoulder, just above knee length satin and silk dress hanging in the wardrobe.

Finally, when looking for his shoes, Tessa brings him a pair of smart black court shoes with red heels, red yes, but noticeably shorter than those that he had become accustomed to wearing.

'Are you sure?'

'These are for you, I would suggest that you put them on and don't ask any questions.'

So Faron dresses as instructed, Gianetta finishes off his makeup. Although she doesn't speak much, he can sense a certain softening in her attitude towards him.

'Shall we go down now?'

'Not tonight Aideen,' Tessa smiles, 'you make your entrance alone.'

'But I need for you two to cover for me coming down the stairs.'

'Oh you can fall down without our help.'

'Tessa!'

' … don't be mean,' Faron and Tessa complete in unison.

'Best of luck Aideen.'

'Thanks Gi. Okay, I'll see you guys on the other side,' and with his head high, shoulders back and back straight, he goes to face his public. *The Faron show continues.*

He starts to descend the golden flecked stairs, there is a large crowd of people in the hallway, milling around and talking. Why they are all there, is, for the moment a mystery for him.

As he starts to take the first few steps, his presence is noticed, the talking stops and everyone turns to watch him make his entrance. – Here is the answer, they have come to see him, he is tonight's star attraction.

Shit, what if I fall now, that would be bloody embarrassing.

However, Aideen is sucking up the attention. Hours of walking up and down stairs, with heels noticeably higher than these have given her the confidence to float down towards them. The confidence translates itself into a wide, relaxed smile.

As she arrives at the foot of the stairs, the Colonel appears from out of the crowd and proffers his arm to the young goddess.

'Good evening, my dear. I must say that you are looking most charming.'

'Thank you Colonel, and you are as debonair as always.' And so they drift off into the ballroom, followed at a respectable distance by the rest of the congregation.

They pass a long moment exchanging inconsequential small talk. All the time, the other guests pass as close as possible, just to confirm that all passes as it should.

There is quite a lot a wine flowing and the Colonel sees to it that they both are well serviced with alcohol. Faron, in a sense, distant and watching, is aware that they are drinking quite a descent quantity, but whether it is due to his drinking habits and constitution, or that of Aideen, they succeed to keep reasonably clear headed.

'Would you be so kind as to find me some titbits to eat, m' dear?'

'My pleasure, Colonel,' and off she goes to the buffet, all eyes following her every move.

He picks up a plate and proceeds to fill it with a selection of delicacies. Each time he has to pick up a fork or a spoon, there is someone watching, checking, noting just how apt Faron is to manipulate the utensil.

Cleaning dozens of forks and spoons with nails twice the length, and then serving at dinner has made this operation a veritable child's play.

'Thank you, what an interesting selection. If you could just pass me my drink. Oh dear, I seemed to have dropped my fork. If you would be so kind.' *Accident, my arse, you did that on purpose.*

Suddenly all other activity ceases, again all eyes are on her.

No problem, head looking forward, back straight, weight mostly on the heels, bend the knees, look down, pick up and straight the legs.

'I will get you a clean fork.' *And so another test is passed. Bring it on, I'm all over you.*

The evening continues with much wine and several subtle tests.

That is until about eleven o'clock, then, as if Moses had chosen to take a short cut through the room, the crowd splits itself into two. As they part towards the two sides of the room, Faron notices that along the length of the room, there is a thinish ribbon, taped to the floor.

'Time for the drunken sluts to walk,' someone shouts, excitedly.

'What is that about?'

'You ladies have to show us how you can still walk a straight line, nothing more.'

Walking a straight line, half pissed, is already tricky, but we are all wearing heels, that is a little more tricky.

Several girls take the challenge with very varying results. Then it is Faron's turn, he approaches the beginning of the line with a certain trepidation. As usual, the presence arrives unexpectedly and unannounced.

'Aideen, remember cleaning the pool ceiling, fix a spot on the far wall, keep your back straight, bend your knees slightly, and glide to the end. *Oui, Maman, merci pour l'astuce.*

Faron looks down at the line, follows it to the end, then further to the facing wall. He notices a particular mark on the wall, and fixes that as the point to which he will direct himself.

He advances towards the ribbon, the room quietens, this must be one of the important tests, well, so be it. Faron smiles to himself; (it seems that Aideen has passed all the responsibility over to him), takes a slow, deep breath, ever so slightly bends his knees, heel to toe, eye on the spot, and forward.

Not taking a moment to look down takes a certain amount of courage, he could be totally off the path, but somehow the silence of the crowd keeps his confidence up.

'Thank you Aideen, you do not need to continue until you reach the wall. I think that you have more the satisfactorily proven that walking a straight line is totally within your competences.'

This was the first time that Faron had ever really felt that his mother was well and truly proud of him. Even if had to wait until she was an Italian Madam, and he, a teenage girl.

'So, Colonel do you concede?'

'Most graciously, M'lady, you are indeed a genius. True to my word, here is the wager,' and he fishes out of his pocket an old, crumpled, one dollar bill.

'Thank, you, I will treasure that. Now to other business, I have located the nurse, she should be arriving shortly.'

Faron then notices that, as much as he was the centre of everyone's attention for the whole evening, since the winning of the bet, he has ceased to exist.

'And here she is.'

Should Faron be surprised to see that the old nurse is no other than Marie Madeleine? Maybe yes, maybe no, but it was definitely, just the same.

'Are you the nurse that brought the sons of the Duke of Burgundy to Venice.'

'Yes, Colonel, that was my mission. And to place them discretely with one or several families.'

'Do you recognise those two boys?' He points to Luiz and Giuseppe who have stopped playing from the point that the nurse has entered.

She walks slowly and a little painfully up to the podium. She then takes her time to look closely at the two young men.

'Yes, yes, they are definitely sons of the Duke.'

'So, which one is the older?'

'Why Symon, of course, he is the older of the two.'

'But which is Symon?' Gianetta can't control her need to know.

'This is Symon,' she points to Giuseppe. Gianetta gasps and sighs, Tessa walks to the drinks table, grabs a bottle of l'eau de vie, and leaves.

'So it's decided then, Giuseppe you are to marry Casilda.'

'Why?'

'I would have thought that you, of all people would know of the betrothal between my daughter and the young Duke.'

'Well, of course I do, what I don't understand is why you think that Symon should be marrying your daughter, as he was never betrothed to her.'

'But of course he was, he is the oldest brother, you've just said so yourself.'

'What I said was Symon is the older of these two brothers.'

'Then it was he that was betrothed to Casilda.'

'Not at all.'

'Please could you be kind enough as to explain a little clearer, we all seem to be a little lost here.' Always in control, my mother.

'Symon is the oldest of these two brothers, but he is not the oldest of the family.'

'So who is?' It was now Aideen that couldn't contain her patience.

'Evrard is the first born.'

'And just where might this, the eldest of the male offspring's be?'

'I'm sorry ma'am, but I lost him.'

'You lost him? You lost the child betrothed to me daughter?'

'I was bringing the children here, the three boys. I had the two little one's in a perambulator, but there was no room for Evrard, so I was carrying him in a handbag.'

'A handbag?'

'Yes ma'am, I must have put it down somewhere while I was looking for my papers, I had just got off the train. And, then, and then,' she starts to weep, 'I forgot it, I forgot the bag with Evrard in it. I of course remembered later, and went back to find it, but it was nowhere to be seen.'

'Wait a minute.'

'What is it Colonel?

'Which railway station are you talking about?'

'Why the station here in Venice, the Marco Polo train station.'

Suddenly Marco rushes in, carrying an old battered bag.

'Is this the bag?' She takes it and very slowly examines it.

'Why yes, yes this is my bag. Where did you get it, young man?'

'He was found in it. I was passing through the station when I saw the baby abandoned there. So I brought it home. As I found him in the Marco Polo station, I named him Marco. Ma'am, is this young man the long lost eldest offspring of the late Duke.'

'Yes, I think that it is.'

'You will need to be sure before I can accept him as the heir.'

Faron finds himself being propelled forward, 'you don't by any chance have a ring that was hung around your neck?'

'You mean this?' And he digs his hand into his shirt collar and draws out a ring, it is identical to the other two.

'Marco, am I to marry you?'

'Only if you want to.'

'Not at all mi'boy, she has no choice, you will marry my daughter.'

'With the greatest of pleasure sir.'

'Girls, I think that everyone should have another drink, it is high time we celebrated. … To the greatest of pleasures. Cin cin!' Faron looks at Kaa, she has hypnotised and manipulated everyone and everything, and for the first time ever, he is proud to be her son.

40. Transition

The sky is clear and the day is warm. Faron and Guida are again benefitting from the Venetian early morning breeze.

'So, what have you learnt from this week?'

'How to walk up and down stairs in heels so high that you can't even have a good time?'

The guide does not even deign to reply to this.

'That by seeking pleasure without caring for the other, will not bring me pleasure.'

'That is good, very good. And what follows that?

'That I have to give up ever experiencing real pleasure, because I just don't deserve it.'

'And you have given up ever deserving having pleasure?'

'I'm just selfish to the bone.'

'I seemed to see you were making great efforts to help solve the girl's problems.'

'It wasn't me, it was Aideen. If it was left to me, I wouldn't have done anything.'

'So you haven't learned anything from your contact with her?'

'What do you mean?'

'You have had a unique opportunity to experience how it is to be in contact with your emotions, and to have an automatic desire to help others. You, Faron have felt, said and done things, even if your own free will wasn't the motor of them.'

'So you think that having cared for them, even if it was Aideen that initiated and directed it, I should have learnt about caring?'

'Would it not be of some use?'

'Yeh, sure, if it was true.'

'Would you like to find out?' They are just about to cross one of the many wooden slat bridges that cross the narrower canals.

'If I am able to care for others? If I might deserve to find and experience pleasure?'

'It might be an interesting experiment.'

'Sure, why not?'

'Then, be careful where you step.'

Faron automatically looks down at his feet. His shoes have suddenly changed into thick wedged flip-flops. His movement also seems to be more restricted, as if he is again wearing the tight stocking over his legs. Even the wooden slats of the narrow hump backed bridge seem slightly different.

Which is, after all, not so very surprising, considering that the small, humped back wooden bridge is only an ornamental addition to a beautifully kept, walled in, Japanese garden.

'Welcome to Japan …'

Gentle reader, thank you for purchasing this book and I very much hope that you have enjoyed it.

If so, please help others to make the choice to read this by sharing your views with your friends and writing a review on Amazon or in any other fashion that you see fit..

http://amzn.to/1KHPjvQ

If you have any other feedback, or would like to contact me, please feel free to leave a comment on my FB page.

https://www.facebook.com/gary.gedall

Thank you,

Kindest regards

Gary

Other Titles

By

Gary Edward Gedall

Island of Serenity Book 1
The Island of Survival

Pierre-Alain James 'Faron' Ferguson is about to commit suicide. In his suicide note he attempts to understand how he has come to have wrecked not only his own life, but also all of those around him.

Pierre-Alain James 'Faron' Ferguson finds himself in a type of 'no-mans-land', between here and there, he must accept to visit the 7 islands before he will be allowed to continue on to his next steps. The islands are named; Survival, Pleasure, Esteem, Love, Expression, Insight and lastly, the Island of Serenity

In this first of a multi volume series, we follow Pierre-Alain through his early years, meeting his parents, brother, nurse and eventually the love of his life.

He also experiences the prehistoric island of Survival, where he must relink with the most basic of human traits.

Join us on a journey that will span all of human consciousness, time and the planet.

Island of Serenity Book 2
Sun & Rain

This is the second chapter of Faron's life history, in which he falls in love, becomes a real cowboy, starts boarding school and finds his two best friends.

He also comes face to face, for the first time of many of the dilemmas and choices of young adult life.

His conflicts and torments start him on the road towards isolation and betrayal.

How would you react, if you were caught on the same lonely road?

Island of Serenity Book 3
The Island of Pleasure vol 2

Faron finds himself in the mystery of a long ago China.

Who is this sad, young man that he must help to find back his pleasure in life?

And how does he end up in the middle of a war that it is impossible for him to participate in?

How will helping others to find pleasure, aid Faron in his own quest towards integrating pleasure into his own life?

Faron then arrives in India; frequently projected into past moments of a young native Indian's life.

While also profoundly experiencing the realities of the present, Faron finally integrates the concept of pleasure into his tortured soul.

Tasty Bites

(Series – published or in preproduction)

Face to Face

A young teacher asks to befriend an older colleague on Face Book, "I have a very delicate situation, for which I would appreciate your advice"

Free 2 Luv

The e-mail exchanges between; RichBitch, SecretLover, the mother, the bestie, and the lawyer, expose a complicated and surprising story

Heresy

An e-mail from a future controlled by the major pharmaceutical companies, "please do what you can to change this situation, now, before it happens …

Love you to death   A toy town parable, populated by
your favourite playthings, about
the dangerous game of dependency
and co-dependency

Master of all Masters   In an ancient land, the
disciples argue about who is the
Master of all Masters. The solution
is to create a competition

Pandora's Box   If you had a magic box, into
which you could bury all
your negative thoughts and
feelings, wouldn't that be
wonderful?

Shame of a family   Being born different can be a
heavy burden to bear.
Especially for the family

The Noble Princess   If you were just a humble
Saxon, would you be good
enough to marry a noble
Norman Princess?

The Ugly Barren Fruit Tree   A weird foreign tree that bears no fruit, in an apple orchard. What value can it possibly have?

The Woman of my Dreams What would you do, if the woman that you fell in love with in your dream, suddenly appears in real life?

None Fiction:

The Zen approach to Low Impact Training and Sports
A simple method for achieving a healthy body and a healthy mind

Many of us approach our fitness and sports activities in an aggressive and competitive fashion.

And even if we feel that we succeed to break out of our comfort zones and win against ourselves or our opponent, there is an important cost to bear.

This level of violence that we have come to accept, so as to reach our goals is also an aggression against ourselves. By removing this need to 'win at any price', and tuning in with our bodies and emotions, we can achieve an enormous amount, all the while being in harmony with our mind, body and spirit.

The Zen approach to Low Impact Training and Sports, is a new softer approach where you can have the best of all worlds.

Adventures with the Master

Dhargey was a sickly child or so his parents treated him.
He was too weak to join the army or work in the fields or even join the
monastery as a normal trainee monk.

To explain to the 'Young Master' why he should be accepted into the order
with a lightened program, he was forced to accompany the revered old man a
little ways up the mountain.

As his parents watched him leave; somewhere they felt that they would never
see their sickly, fragile boy ever again, somewhere they were totally right.

He was a happy, healthy seven year old until he witnessed the riders, dressed
in red and black, destroying his village and murdering his parents; the trauma
cut deep into his psyche.

Only the chance meeting with a wandering monk could set him back onto the
road towards health and serenity.

Through meditation, initiations, stories, taming wild horses, becoming a
monkey, mastering the staff and the sword; the future 'Young Master'
prepares to face his greatest demon.

Two men, two journeys, one goal.

REMEMBER

Stories and poems for self-help and self-development based on techniques of
Ericksonian and auto-hypnosis

*Dusk falls, the world shrinks little by little into a smaller and smaller circle
as the light continues to diminish.*
*The centre of this world is illuminated by a small, crackling sun; the flames
dance, and the rough faces of the people gathered there are lit by the fire of
their expectations.*
*The old man will begin to speak, he will explain to them how the world is,
how it was, how it was created. He will help them understand how things
have a sense, an order, a way that they need to be.*
*He will clarify the sources of un-wellness and unhappiness, what is sickness,
where it comes from, how to notice it and... how to heal it.*
*To heal the sick, he will call forth the forces of the invisible realms, maybe
he will sing, certainly he will talk, and talk, and talk.*

Since the beginning of time we have gathered round those who can bring
us the answers to our questions and the means to alleviate our sufferings.
This practice has not fundamentally changed since the earliest times; in
every era, continent and culture we have found and continue to find these
experiences.

In this, amongst the oldest of the healing traditions, he has succeeded to meld
modern therapy theories and techniques with stories and poems of the highest
quality.

With much humanity, clinical vignettes, common sense and lots of humour,
the reader is gently carried from situation to situation. Whether the problems
described concern you directly, indirectly or not at all, you will surely find
interest and benefits from the wealth of insights and advices contained within
and the conscious or unconscious positive changes through reading the stories
and poems.

The Tales of
Peter the Pixie

Peter the innocent, honest, young pixie, and his friends; Elli, the, 'much older then she looks', modest but powerful Fairy, Timothy, the old, trustworthy, Toad and the, ever so noble, Fire Dragon, are the best of friends.

Together, they experience many wonderful and heart-warming adventures.

Told in a classical children's story style; Peter and his friends, meet all kinds of creatures and situations.

As with all children, Peter is often confronted with experiences that he does not know how best to deal with, and he often reacts in ways that are not the most appropriate. Fortunately; with the help of his good friends, good will and common sense, everything always turns out for the best.

Picturing the Mind

A simple, single model, accessible to everyone, to explain the development, functioning and dis-functioning of the human psyche.

For the common man and woman in the street, the complex and competing theories and models of the human psyche; its development, functioning and dis-functioning are often unhelpful for their understanding of themselves.

This becomes even more problematic when they find themselves in difficulty, as often, even the mental health professionals, who are experts in their own fields, find themselves at a loss to communicate successfully how and why the patent is unwell and what needs to happen to find or regain a healthy balance.

This opens up the question; 'is it possible to image a simple, single model, accessible to everyone, to explain the development, functioning and dis-functioning of the human psyche?'

One that builds on existing theories and models, benefitting from the mass of experience and research of 'modern western' psychological concepts and ideas, but also integrating traditional visions of the human psyche and modern theories from the physical sciences.

Picturing the Mind, is an attempt to answer to this need.

www.ingramcontent.com/pod-product-compliance
Lightning Source LLC
Chambersburg PA
CBHW071359300726

48976CB00006B/1930